THE MAUSOLEUM OF GORE

Also by Jonathan Raab

Project Vampire Killer

The Haunting of Camp Winter Falcon

The Crypt of Blood: A Halloween TV Special

The Hillbilly Moonshine Massacre

Jonathan Raab

Illustrations by Mat Fitzsimmons
Cover and title art by Trevor Henderson

ISBN: 979-8-9879688-4-0

Edited by Steve Grinstead

Illustrations by Mat Fitzsimmons

Cover and title art by Trevor Henderson

Ravenscroft typeface © Justin Callaghan.
Used under commercial license.

Double Feature typeface © David Shetterly.
Used under the SIL Open Font License.

Joystix Monospace typeface by Typodermic.

Published by Muzzleland Press
Victor, NY

For Leif Jonker, Joe Meredith,
and Brian Paulin

BROADCASTER'S DISCLAIMER

Colored bars, stacked over a row of grey gradients in test pattern, give way to a wash of static and a piercing, shrill hum. The speakers snap. The screen falls into darkness for a slim moment, allowing a brief glimpse of your phantom reflection in its flat, black void. Before you can register the details of your own face—and of the tall, looming figure standing menacingly behind you—a field of soft blue emerges from the abyss, home to white text writ in a sterile, blocky typeface. It was generated in outdated software once sold to secondary Canadian television markets for weather updates and to public access stations in the American Rust Belt to create title cards.

This fuzzy text is prologue to the amateur assemblage that is *The Mausoleum of Gore*, preserved in the H.264-encoded MP4 file playing on your personal computer. Is this echo of the analog past just part of *The Mausoleum of Gore*'s original presentation, or was it added later by an archivist, a torrenter tagging their source, or an overzealous, unofficial contributor to the TV special and its legacy?

Perhaps the incoherence is all part of the show.

The text scrolls by, slowly but surely, inviting you

to squint to read it all, demanding the audience not merely be a passive observer, but an active participant:

WARNING

The following contains scenes of explicit violence, gore, and subversive messages about civil authorities. Only those with deranged minds and warped morals should stay up late to watch this presentation of THE MAUSOLEUM OF GORE, and only in secret. Complaints to the degenerate wizards of the FCC will be met with hostility and overwhelming force. Tattletales who bring in busybody parents and reactionary community activists will find themselves buried alive, their screaming mouths filled in by the soil of shallow graves dug in haste by blood-stained hands and bent-blade shovels. Rusty knives have been slid across throats and screams drowned in rushing blood for lesser offenses. Your particular crimes are known to us, whispered about and giggled over in the deep places and dark holes of the nearby and ever-present Woods. You know EXACTLY what and where we mean, you son of a bitch.

The Broadcaster and this program's gracious Sponsors assume no responsibility for the film's content, its political ramifications, or the imminent psycho-spiritual infections that will soon traverse your blood-brain barrier [IF YOU'VE MADE IT THIS FAR, IT'S ALREADY TOO LATE]. The consequences of this molecular-level shift may be occluded by the rote buzzing of despair under present material conditions [AND YOUR VARIOUS SUBSTANCE ABUSE ADDICTIONS AND EMBARRASSING PERSONAL/MENTAL HEALTH ISSUES] for but a short while, until they are inevitably revealed through uncontrollable urges manifested in the swing of an axe against a pliant neck, the revealing of diseased tissue by a twisted silver knife, or the guttural grinding of a chainsaw blade set to work on skull plate. What fun awaits you and your loved ones!

This film is for Halloween fun-fun good times and educational purposes only. The producers are not liable for any BLOODY OCCULT RITUAL that may commence after PSYCHOTRONIC DATA has been absorbed by your subconscious and synthesized into actionable crimes by your malformed spirit. The filmmakers responsible [REPREHENSIBLE!] for THE MAUSOLEUM OF GORE are lay practitioners of the dark art of CINÉMA GOBLIN, clumsily wielding supernatural power with malicious intent to create video entertainment products for content-craving audiences committed to self-destructive attitudes of ironic detachment [GHASTLY PUKE NOISES].

The effects of willingly engaging with THE MAUSOLEUM OF GORE are akin to drinking from the witches' brew straight out of the cauldron, easing into undeath with the teeth of the vampire embedded in your neck, or being scared to death by a glowing green skeleton in a dark sublevel of a haunted mansion: immensely pleasurable on some sub-erotic valence, triggering a release of endorphins and hormones associated with your deepest, most innocent, and yet deeply primal delights. How might one tear a hole through time and space? Well, ingestion and excretion of the consumer and the consumed, an ouroboros of sign/signifier/signified-audience co-creation of meaning using the raw materials of creaky old Gothic horror movies and slasher film garbage might just do the trick. If the author is dead ["AND WE CERTAINLY ARE!" SHOUT THE LEERING SKELETONS AND VILE GOBLINS WHO SUMMONED THIS TEXT INTO BEING], then so is the audience. Let us enjoy this season for the dead, for us, together.

This is not a work of fiction, in the sense that all stories are alive, and that history is constructed and reanimated out of the living remains of the dead, assembled and made to live, again, by the blood-soaked survivors or perpetrators of unspeakable crimes who, operating purely out of autonomic instinct or death-drive, wish to create their very own Monster. Their [OUR/YOUR] stories are built from memories assembled over time and warped in the searing heat of traumatic events and shadow, shouted down the echoing tunnel of pain that is humankind's bloody and insane evolutionary and social history.

When will God turn His face from the horrors of His children and say, "Enough is enough"? We're still waiting for someone to pull the plug on the tasteless horror movie that began the moment when clay became flesh, when primordial chemical soup organized into cells, when some great and terrible crime was perpetrated on some poor ape, granting it self-awareness and the imaginative capacity for lies and murder and worse.

If you are of sound mind and body, you will not willingly participate, nor allow others to participate through your own inaction, in the viewing of this slime-ridden spookshow. If you are of legal age and lucky enough to live within a polity in which cannabis is legal to consume [HOW CAN THIS BE? WHEN WAS THIS FILM/BOOK PRODUCED, OR WHEN WAS IT SUPPOSED TO HAVE BEEN PRODUCED? WHO IS IN CHARGE OF THIS OPERATION?], we recommend that you do so now, early and often, in order to mitigate the damaging psychic effects of living under that dread *vampyr*, Capital, and that you get extra-super-duper high to maximize your reaction to the vibrant colors and fog effects presented as the Halloween, autumnal, atmospheric feel-good vibes of this production.

You are going to die.
WE ARE ALREADY DEAD.
Viewer discretion is advised.

Black.
Blurry, blocky computer typeface:

THE MAUSOLEUM OF GORE

PRODUCED BY A LOCAL CABAL OF
GHOSTS & GOBLINS

FUNDED IN PART BY A GENEROUS
CREATIVES GRANT PROVIDED BY
MALTHUS CORPORATION,
INTERNATIONAL ARTS AND
SCIENCES PHILANTHROPIC TRUST

Eruption

A static line cuts across the title card like the jagged slash of a killer's knife across a virginal throat. It lingers as a lightning strike stuck in time—growing larger, wider, until it envelops the whole screen, until the electronic wound becomes the totality of awareness, of being, of reality.

But then, as the ember of a dying fire might suddenly catch the wind and return to life, recognizable patterns of light and sound emerge. From within the folds of distortion, vibrant colors of a valley in autumnal splendor are revealed. Proud bouquets of leaves are held aloft by great branches. Crimson covers the hills in great slashes, blood dribbling through patches of cloudburst orange and smears of putrefied yellow, all set beneath a gravestone-grey sky. Barren trees are the hands of revenants grasping at the sky from brooding hills and lonely valleys laden with creeping tributaries of fog.

This is October Country. The true time and place of harvest and All Souls and Halloween, always with us, always present, even when hidden under the pallor of winter's funeral shroud, forgotten beneath the saccharine touch of the young lover, spring, or occluded by the vulgar beauty of summer.

Errant lines of distortion mark the footage, and the handheld shots waver and vibrate. Digital artifacts, the odd visual warp, and recorded-over images emerge like ghosts and disappear just as quickly, shadows of radiation implying inhuman forms and the garbled voices of the dead. A subtle, ever-present audio hiss is noticeable whenever a cut occurs, even over the droning John Carpenter–knockoff synthesizer score that lingers on its notes for uncomfortably long stretches, as if the music was recorded onto a cassette tape exposed to the sun for too long.

The visual and aural degradation produce a sense that this "TV Special" was created by those whose vision exceeded their capabilities. These characteristics are not cheap post-production visual effects clumsily applied to otherwise clean digital footage. Given that there has been no effort to clean up the picture or the sound, maybe these effects were left in, on purpose, as part of the aesthetic identity of the production. Perhaps medium *is* the message, imperfections and all. Or, perhaps the filmmakers didn't know any better, and you give them entirely too much credit, because you find the imperfections both charming and comforting in some undefined, nostalgia-infected manner, or because they work to create an abstract *mood* of unease and atmosphere that something captured in high definition and sanitized simply could not.

Crumbling county highways lead to Dutch-angle horizon points. Bullet-ridden deer crossing signs are crooked pikes in moist earth. An old barn stands away from the road, its stone foundation and walls disintegrating in genuflection toward the haunted hills. Rotting wooden fenceposts hold up rusty strands of barbed wire. Fields laden with cornstalks wait beneath the grey sky. Mailboxes stand at uncomfortable angles before dirt driveways. Rail lines crisscross roads and snake through dark stretches of swamp. Great industrial buildings of locally sourced stone are overgrown with strange vegetation along the Erie Canal, whose slate-grey waters are almost still.

The canal parallels the state route that leads into Canaltown, a village embedded within great swaths of trees—some colorful, others bare, and many simply dead, rendered unto memorial by the plague-touch of invasive species. Houses appear from the fog: a mix of Colonials and Victorians falling into varying states of disrepair, with flaking roofs and faded paint but showing signs of life (or *undeath*, as it were) via colorful Halloween decorations.

Homemade ghosts flap their white sheets in the soft wind, hanging from desiccated trees; cardboard gravestones painted grey and black stand adorned with jokey names like "A.W. Itch," "Gary G. Ghoul," "Frederick K. Ruger," and so on. Black rubber bats hang from soffits and porch roofs. Colorful fabric witches ride brooms or are comically spattered against telephone poles. Doors are covered in crinkly plastic depictions of movie psycho-murderers, pumpkin-headed scarecrow men, or ominous phantoms. Plastic skeletons—sitting on rocking chairs, shackled to support beams—laugh with jaws hanging open at some joke long gone to rot. Great paper faces of vampires, Frankensteinian horrors, wart-faced witches, skulls with glowing yellow eyes, black cats, and more leer from windows. Straw-stuffed zombies climb over sagging picket fences, reaching for the slow stream of traffic passing by.

Some of the houses display more modest, harvest-festival fare: a clutch of pumpkins huddled close against the cold; smiling, kid-friendly scarecrows bedecked in bright autumnal oranges and greens; ears of corn lashed to mailboxes and gates. While these are acceptable offerings to the ghosts, goblins, and ghouls, the eye tends to slide away from the cute and onto the horrific, where it lingers with a mix of repulsion and desire, as the rites and true spirit of the season are understood by our very anatomy. The eye finds what the heart desires.

Farther on, downtown, is a mix of storefronts, more of them empty this year than last: a lawyer's office, a dental practice, mayfly coffee shops, restaurants, breweries advertising regional beers in neon signage. Heading south out of town, the barely-out-of-the-way grey-market cannabis dispensary offers discounts on horror movie–themed flower. Hockey Mask Killer Cush, Pet Semetary Sativa, and Dracula Dank are all quite popular this season, even if they are simply re-branded versions of standard offerings. If one desires a truly spooktacular high, only a select few strains will do. The King in Yellow has recently arrived in upstate New York, offering divine revelation of the stage play we all unwillingly and unwittingly inhabit, glimpses of the dead spiral-city at the place beyond time (the end of the performance, so to speak), and a pleasant, full-body high. Rest assured, the filmmakers of this particular sorcerous act of the Cinema Goblin school of filmmaking are well versed in the kiss of the King, and his smoke infuses every digital frame and every square pixel of this lo-fi production.

Up on the great hill that looms over the village, the suburban-cut stretches of wider streets and generous plots of well-kept lawns are home to houses where full-size candy bars are more likely to be found. Twelve-foot skeleton giants leer from behind fences or dominate front yards, symbols of avarice but also of reckless Halloween spirit, so Mammon's sin is forgivable in this case. Inflatable, cutesy ghouls and ghosts wave in the breeze, kept afloat by buzzing electric fans. Housecats left to roam, eyes red and alive with mischief, scurry from shadow to shadow, eager for the sun to set and the night's fun to begin. Painted pumpkins and gourds tastefully adorn some of the ghoul-free houses. Jack o'lanterns wait patiently for their time to glow.

The cemetery is laid out just opposite the school campus, acres of gravestones standing in silent contrast to the pulsing rhythms of early life that flow throughout the district's great brick buildings. The grounds of the dead are well kept, with neat rows of white stones and markers whose names, dates, and epitaphs remain readable, and whose immediate areas are often visited by the living.

But there is also the darker, more distant back section, held within the shadow of the trees that press in from the low hills beyond. There the remaining plots are cheaper, the footpaths grow muddy and overgrown, the gravestones crowd together in clusters like mold or cancer cells. We will return here, shortly, but for now, let this stretch of soil and death linger in your memory like the aftertaste of smoke from a great, pre-Christian bonfire, set ablaze in the deepest reaches of a dark, central European forest.

On the edge of town is the small college campus, Canaltown's lifeblood—and its curse. The walkways that snake between the brick monoliths are empty, save for the scattered leaves that flutter about in flocks pushed into the air by unsteady gusts of wind. The canal rushes by, its footpaths home to local residents out for an evening stroll. Fog creeps up to the footpaths from the trees, rendering the scene Gothic in tone, and therefore ideal.

Following the water, we find the derelict industrial core, home to storage silos and workhouses collapsing under the accumulated weight of decades of deindustrialization. Faded logos and labor recruitment ads stick stubbornly to the brick facades, drawing in ghosts with the promise of a prosperity and upward mobility that no longer exists. Instead of workers and aspirants to the middle class, this place now only attracts trouble: kids and teenagers looking for something to smash or a place to drink and smoke and who-knows-what-else; vermin looking for a place to writhe and procreate; aggressive coyotes and raptors looking for a defensible alcove into which they might drag their wounded prey.

The canal winds more closely into this section of town. Towering over the water here is the great metal superstructure that serves as canal lock, its bronze armor having turned green in the long decades since its utility. It stretches across the waterway, the lock door raised high to let small boats pass beneath. The metal moans in the soft wind, and on lonely nights its creaking and shifting are harsh notes sung in despair.

The film's establishing shots having done their work well, the change begins with the music. An adjustment of tenor, of tone, a downward slide into ominous notes. The great lock dissolves into a slow, surprisingly smooth dolly-in down a wide residential street, the wind whipping clusters of fallen leaves into vortexes of color. Handmade ghosts made of tissue paper hang from fishing line and bob in the breeze, bearing witness to the conflagration just now beginning to unfold.

Further dissolves bring us to a tree. Wide and muscular, old and resplendent, with a weary crown of red leaves still clinging to its topmost branches. Behind it, just out of focus, is a house with a porch that is home to a full extended family of jack o'lanterns, their dreadful grins lit by sputtering candles of fresh flame as the sun sinks behind the nearby hills.

There is a postproduction sound effect: a wet, sliding *snap* like a kitchen knife slicing through a head of fresh lettuce, and a sharp cut to a close-up of the old tree's bark or, rather, molding made to appear as bark, spray-painted brown and grey, the smell of paint and rubber having lingered in the garage in which it was applied, becoming a permanent sense memory.

The rubber bark splits open along thinly sliced fissures, and from within pulses a neon-orange substrate, muscle seeking escape from a prison of skin. A great heartbeat, laden with reverb and underpinned by ominous synth-organ notes, slowly beats its errant rhythm. The soundtrack is alive with the hiss and pop of splitting bark—or at least of splitting vegetables—wet and crisp, and the street is full of these eruptions, these veins of bright orange exploding out from trees that should be settling in for their long winter-season rest but are instead remade into mockeries of their former shapes by this inexplicable, candy-colored infection.

As the sky grows darker, the orange tissues that pop up in discolored veins radiate a dreadful light that suffuses the neighborhood with a complementary seasonal ambiance, one attuned to an imminent apocalypse of Halloween vibrancy.

Beneath the street, the earth rumbles and shakes. A Christopher Lee–inspired vampire blow-mold topples over. Leaves shake loose from trees. A black cat watches from the shadows, its eyes reflecting the strange fire of glowing orange light. Blacktop gives way to stone forms that emerge from the depths of the earth, the camera shaking vigorously to disguise the method of special effect, whether practical or digital. The face of an angel pushes through crumbling pavement, hands raised toward heaven in a cry for mercy for the sinners of the world. Small rectangular grave markers follow, then full-on headstones, driving up toward the grey sky. Parts of the street, the sidewalk, and yards erupt with spear-pointed metal spikes, followed swiftly by metal pillars and grey columns of fence and stretches of bone-white stone wall. A reflecting pool slams up through the surface of the world, splitting as it is revealed, dry as bleached bone.

White stone crypts—stained black and brown by soil and mold—shed dirt and asphalt as they jump up and out, shaking and shifting from explosive pressures. Fresh caskets and decayed wooden coffins poke their corners up from the disturbed topsoil. Angels and saints, Mothers Mary and great crosses and crucifixes, Stars of David and solemn black stone markers of the irreligious, grand markers of the wealthy and the humblest of rust-ridden metal plates; tombs and mausoleums, family ossuaries and beggars' rows—together, all are emergent, unveiled from subterranean occlusion.

The rich and the poor and the in-between, the faithful and the unfaithful, the meek and the willful, are all rendered as one in death, their lives reduced to quiet displays of stone and metal and rot, here, finally, on Main Street, in a small town in Gothic upstate New York.

Trunk or Treat Carnival Promo #1

The audio track pops, and a barrage of images cycles through the screen: a color-bar test pattern; an American flag flapping in the sunset in 4:3 aspect ratio; an ambulance pulling away from the charred remains of an oversized pickup truck on the side of the road; a news clip of a man clutching a small bundle of bone and blood, tears streaming down his face. Beneath it all is a field-hum of static and a rhythmic electronic pulse.

A synthesized feminine voice, barely audible, repeats a strange prayer: *one, six, alpha, bravo, five, beta, three, two, two. One, six, alpha, bravo, five, beta, three, two, two...*

A flashlight, held outward by a pair of shaking hands, points into the dark of a barn, where shadows and dust swirl.

Two men, draped with animal skins, one adorned with antlers, under a swirling sky of alien stars.

A group of people in black robes, gathered in a narrow basement.

A planchette sliding across a wooden spirit board toward *NO*.

Snapping audio and a cut to stock footage captured in the haze of decades past: a row of smiling jack o'lanterns with clumsy candlelit smiles; kids in plastic-smock and plastic-mask costumes at a doorway, begging for candy; smiling clowns making animal balloons; children in black vampire capes bobbing for apples; food carts and games of skill and chance and more.

A radio-announcer voice, out of time:

"...a safe and well-lit place to take the whole family! Patronize one of the many Chamber of Commerce businesses to get your tickets for the big giveaway. Bubuo the Clown and his merry band of pranksters will be performing magic tricks and espousing the benefits of center-right austerity economics in our present era of societal despair and psychic collapse. The event is free to all residents of Canaltown. Poor families from outside the village proper must bring proof of local purchase to gain entrance to the carnival. Event co-sponsored by the Staff and Employee Council of Malthus Aeronautics and Guidance Systems Site 322, just down the 90. Meet the brave men and women on the front lines of weapons industry R&D and get a free secondhand book fished out of the dumpster after the last Friends of the Library sale.

"See the SUNY Canaltown Police tactical SWAT RV command center, an MRAP armored vehicle, and men and women in tactical body armor and black face masks and helmets carrying M4 rifles. No, you haven't inadvertently wandered into some resource rich Third World territory—our imperial wars have come home, and in a big way!

"The middle school band will be collecting cans to fundraise for mold mitigation in the practice hall.

"This is an all-ages, faith-based community event, and not in any way associated with the pagan idolatry of Halloween..."

A shot of a bulldozer, pushing a mound of charred bodies into an open grave. In contrast to the stock local news channel footage that precedes it, this shot is (impossibly, considering how old *The Mausoleum of Gore* is) of current events. Maybe someone edited it in as a joke or editorialization.

Sure.

The electronic voice re-emerges from static, just before the image of the atrocity evaporates: *one, six, alpha, bravo, five, beta, three, two, two. One, six, alpha, bravo, five, beta, three, two, two...*

Channel 3 Rochester News on the Scene

The texture of the film/reality changes. Details are crisper. The blacks are blacker. Light sources trail into tiny will-o'-wisps that disintegrate into a haze of digital artifacts: streetlights, glowing jack o'lanterns, the bright headlights and taillights of cars stuck in their narrow driveways along Main Street. That stretch of pavement is now a necropolis, full of jagged stones, open crypts, half-buried gargoyles, and the statuary of saints and angels reaching toward heaven. All is illuminated by the candy corn-orange glow emanating from split-open trees.

Children in costumes and teenagers in hoodies dart among the inexplicable wreckage, leaping over headstones, posing with dirt-encrusted statues for selfies, shooting videos of their friends leaping from atop familial tombs down to the dark, disturbed earth.

YOLANDA SALAZAR
CHANNEL 3 ROCHESTER FIELD REPORTER
"Plenty of communities in the Rochester area take Halloween seriously, going all out with decorations, trick-or-treating, spooky haunted houses, and so on.

But Canaltown, just southwest of the city, has taken holiday *spirit* to a whole new level."

Salazar stands before the roundabout on the southeast side of town, her pumpkin-orange sport coat and skirt accented by pinstripes of green and black. Her hair is long, black, and lustrous, and her large, beautiful brown eyes compete for frame space against the carnage of crypts and caskets beyond.

"Someone's idea of a Halloween prank has gotten a little out of hand," she continues in her carefully modulated mid-Atlantic TV accent, not missing a beat. "Grave markers, headstones, tombs, statues, crosses, stars, even stretches of stone wall and wrought iron fence—all of these things have exploded out of the folds of the earth up and down this stretch of Main Street. I spoke to many residents of Canaltown this afternoon, trying to get to the bottom of this macabre mystery."

NINA VAN HORN
VILLAGE COUNCIL

A woman in a conservative business dress stands on the sidewalk, the muted, dark blues of her suit standing in contrast to the vibrant oranges, greens, and purples of the Halloween decorations arrayed on the porch immediately behind her, just out of focus. She is middle aged, with her long hair pulled back into a bun, her dark dress suit absorbing the bright light of the camera crew's rig that floods the area. Others gather behind her, faces pale and gaunt under the TV lights.

"None of this is cause for alarm, really," Van Horn says, matter-of-factly. "It's just some sort of sick gag, played by college students on the residents of our fine town. Anti-American agitators making some sort of clumsy political statement, and using the devil's holiday to do so."

"Those appear to be real grave markers and structures, made from real stone," Salazar responds. "How could a few college kids do this? It would take a crew of heavy equipment operators hours, maybe days, to do this much damage. Didn't anyone notice anything?"

"There's plenty of local color out here for you to interview," Van Horn says with distaste rolling off her tongue. "I'm told the town police and county sheriff's office are looking into the matter." She looks straight into the camera and leans in close to the microphone, causing distortion when she speaks. "There will be prosecutions."

"Do you think the Halloween carnival should be canceled tonight?" Salazar asks, pulling back her microphone.

The councilwoman shakes her head.

"First of all, it is *not* a Halloween carnival, as the village of Canaltown does not recognize Halloween as a formal holiday, and any expenditures made to mark such an occasion would of course be met with the full litigious force of concerned religious parties and parents' groups who make themselves heard at council meetings, parent-teacher association gatherings, school board meetings, library story hours, and the interior spaces of my mind at odd hours of the night, when the whole world is quiet as death and I have only my anxieties about my past mistakes and my paranoia about *being under judgment* to keep me company until strange lights and noises rouse me from my peaceless slumber. Tonight, we are hosting a Trunk or Treat event—specifically as a counterpoint to the vile celebration of evil that you call Halloween, which is in fact the devil's bacchanal."

"But Halloween has multicultural origins, including Christian traditions of charity and veneration of the saints—"

The councilwoman's mouth tightens into an uncanny smile, and she leans in closer to the reporter, the lights casting an unpleasant sheen over her wide forehead.

"That's just woke excuse-making. We all *know* that it's an evil celebration, and our Trunk or Treat event is *wholesome* and *pure* and suitably Satan-free."

"But with the streets full of graves and this strange orange light, maybe you should consider—"

The councilwoman turns toward the camera directly.

"I want to speak to the people of Canaltown, and to the whole Rochester metro area: Come on out! Come enjoy the festivities! Visit our local restaurants, go shopping at one of our many boutique stores selling soaps and candles and legally distinct Buffalo football team merchandise. This is a night for fun, not for horror, and all are welcome to celebrate. There will be food, games, prizes, and live music from 5:30 to 9 p.m. Thank you."

The councilwoman walks away from the glow of the lights.

REGGIE "HOWIE" WITZER
UNEMPLOYED

A man in his late 30s sits in a folding lawn chair, an open green can of Genny Cream Ale balanced on his thigh. He wears a black trucker mesh cap with "AFGHANISTAN WAR VETERAN" emblazoned across the front. His left arm is a prosthetic—all metal, fleshy looking plastic, and intricate mechanisms. The replacement hand clutches a cigarette that he occasionally raises to his lips.

"Are you concerned about the cemetery that has inexplicably appeared in the middle of Main Street?" Salazar asks.

"I mean, sure, I guess, but hopefully they'll have all this cleared outta here by tomorrow," Witzer says, blowing out smoke.

"Who?"

"The village, or the town. Probably the county snowplows could do the job."

"Those are stone markers, and the earth has been greatly disturbed. It may take days or weeks to clear the area, let alone to rebuild the road."

"That's America for ya."

"How's that?"

"Business-connected interests reduce tax revenue and create multiple veto-point procedures to reduce the efficacy of public institutions, all while leveraging resentment of the poor, the queer, the minority, and the immigrant. Those institutions are unable to adequately respond in times of crisis—such as in our present moment—thereby further eroding trust in the public good, and reducing what's left of the commons."

"You think this is political?" Salazar asks, caught off guard.

"Everything is political, ma'am."

"A graveyard appearing in the middle of the road is political?"

"It's a cemetery, because it's not adjacent to a church. But yeah, seems like an awfully loaded symbolic statement of some sort, don't it? I ain't cracked its meaning, if it has one, quite yet. But I'm gonna keep trying." Reggie takes another sip from his can of Genny Cream Ale, then looks up, directly at the camera. "Where are my manners? You guys want a beer?"

MATT STILLWURTER
SMALL BUSINESS OWNER

Cut to a man with a close-shaved head and wraparound black sunglasses, despite the late time of day. He is leaning out of the open driver's-side window of his oversized black pickup truck. His American flag T-shirt is a garish mess of color and lines. The truck is half pulled up onto the sidewalk, idling at an awkward angle.

"The roads are hazardous to drive on," the reporter says. "Aren't you concerned?"

"Ain't hazardous if you've got four-wheel drive!" he shouts, before revving the truck's diesel engine. Black smoke pours out of the tailpipe, then drifts between them. The reporter coughs out a follow-up question.

"But what about the kids out trick-or-treating?"

"If their parents care about them, they won't get hurt," Stillwurter says. "And if they do, that's just survival of the fittest. America needs a little bit more of that these days, if you ask me. These damn millennials need to toughen up!"

"Judging by your age, aren't you a mill—?"

The pickup suddenly lurches forward and Salazar jumps back. The vehicle cuts sharply right, up onto the stone debris and upturned earth in the street, then bounces away from the sidewalk at an awkward angle. The truck slams against headstones and an overturned familial tomb. Metal-on-metal grinding signals the separation of some critical mechanism from its undercarriage. Stone presses against panels and doors, leaving trailing marks as metal groans and gives. The truck shudders to a halt.

Stillwurter leans out of the driver's-side window, a wave of *bleeps* judiciously edited over his profanity. Dark liquid gushes out from beneath the truck, thick fuel dribbling onto the earth and the markers of the dead. Fire spreads up from the underside of the truck as the man struggles to open the door, which is pinned shut against a tall and immobile headstone. His screams are hoarse and panicked.

JADEN PHILLIPSON
GAS STATION ATTENDANT

"Yeah, I seent a UFO," says a young, unshaven man in a drawn-up hoodie. A hand-rolled joint moves back and forth across his hand, over and under his fingers with impressive precision.

"I'm sorry?" Salazar says.

"That's what started all this," Phillipson says. "They tend to precede apocalyptic events. Strange signs and wonders in the heavens." He turns to point behind him, off camera. "I saw it when I was walking home from the park, just a ways south of Route 96. I was smoking some of that new weed my man Tracy got from his son-in-law from Colorado. Called it 'The King in Yellow.' Grown in the soil of a field touched by a meteorite sent by a space god."

"You were intoxicated and you saw a UFO," Salazar says, flatly. "Don't you think that might make your sighting easily explainable?"

"Did you know that they found THC residue atop an altar at the Judahite Shrine of Arad, dating back to around 700 BCE?[1] The priests of the era may have been inhaling cannabis smoke before entering the Holy of Holies. That is, to be in the presence of God, on some level, may have required the use of cannabis, or cannabis facilitated communion, maybe through ritual cleansing of the mind and body."

"What does that have to do with your UFO?"

"What is an unidentified flying object, when spoken of as a 'UFO' specifically, but a harbinger of wonder, a messenger of the spirit world, a portent of strange events to come? I subscribe not to the nuts 'n bolts theory of ufology, but to a more metaphysical, personal, spiritual explanation."

Phillipson pauses to bring the joint to his lips, then sparks a match. Salazar waits patiently as he takes a series of puffs and waves out the match, tossing it onto the lid of an exhumed sarcophagus.

"I don't believe they are here to harvest our DNA and the government knows about it, or other such claptrap. The creatures described in abduction and

---

[1] Eran Arie, Baruch Rosen, and Dvory Namdar, *Cannabis and Frankincense at the Judahite Shrine of Arad, Tel Aviv* 47:1 (2020), 5–28, DOI: 10.1080/03344355.2020.1732046.

third-kind encounters are likely the fey—interdimensional fairies or goblins—not visitors from another planet using what appears to be twentieth-century medical techniques to conduct unnecessarily invasive and outmoded surgeries on confused and terrified white people.

"I speak of the *high strange* in a luminous, religious sense, ma'am. Thus, *I seent a UFO*, a glowing red crystal with a swirling, radioactive halo, not unlike Ezekiel's wheel—perhaps the throne of God itself—and it terrified me, shocked me. It made me want to be a better man, to be a better neighbor, to take the teachings of the Christ and the Buddha and the various prophets seriously. I have felt spiritually charged since the encounter, the capital-E *Encounter* that upended my sense of self and purpose.

"I work at a gas station, ma'am. I have no career prospects and no aspirations beyond saving up for a new video game console or a car or becoming romantically involved with a person of great inner and outward beauty. Why would such a thing of wonder and terror appear to *me*? Well, it prepared me. For this." Phillipson points out at the street, smoke trailing up from the joint. "It prepared me to see the wonder in all of this. The impossible terror. A graveyard in a street."

"Cemetery," Yolanda says.

Jaden nods. "Right."

"Wow."

"Yeah. Wow."

ROXETTE WOOLER
SOCCER MOM / HOMEMAKER

A mom stands with her costumed children at her sides, hugging close and looking straight into the camera. The woman's dyed red and purple hair glimmers in the crew's harsh lights, lines under her eyes all the more exaggerated.

"I sometimes suspect that when we die there is nothing, that we are not going to see God, or that we are not all pieces of God, but that the universe is an unfeeling, un-self-aware machine, oblivious to its own suffering," Wooler says. "Dumbly churning out terror and pain for itself."

"Is that what this event makes you think?" Salazar asks. "That we're alone when we die?"

"That can't possibly be true, can it?" Wooler asks, her eyes wet. "That doesn't feel right, but yes, sometimes I fear that may be the case. That eternity after death is suffocation."

"Dreadful," Salazar says, nonchalant, moving the microphone down to the costumed little girl, who is wrapped in white fabric that is ominously stained red. "What are you dressed up as for Halloween?"

"I'm a school shooting victim," she says, two of her front teeth missing in her uneven smile.

[NAMETAGS REMOVED AND BADGE
NUMBERS BLACKED OUT]

A shot of two police cars, flashing lights illuminating the street, casting crimson along the gathered faces of the people of Canaltown. The cars are parked on the hill leading down to the traffic roundabout that sits at the edge of the village. The trees in its center have been supplanted by jagged headstones and stone angels locked in reverent prayer. The cops stand in front of their cars, shaking their heads at the mess of stonework and disturbed earth making the road impassable.

"Officers, would you be able to shed some light on—"

"Get that [*bleep*] camera out of my face." One of them moves forward, left hand up to cup the camera lens, the other reaching for his gun.

WALT CARRERA
RETIRED

"They say the devil comes out on Halloween but there ain't no devil," Carrera says, his dull blue eyes staring through Yolanda, his face marked with the ravages of age, his remaining hair thin and insubstantial over a pale patch of skin stretched taut along the top of his skull. "There's only the cruel and sinful heart of man."

He pauses, his eyes refocusing, as if remembering where he is, who he is. "There ain't no devil, but I saw something like as much, if there could ever be a thing. I seen something like a man that weren't no man, crawling on all fours along the railroad tracks that run through town. It was on a night when the moon was high and the fog clung low, and seeing how them limbs moved and bent in ways impossible, it gave me a fright, and it made me rethink what I once thought I knew about the world."

"But what about the graves in the street?"
Carrera shrugs.
"I got no idea what this is all about."

DANIEL AND JOHNNY MING
STUDENTS AT SUNY CANALTOWN

Daniel is a vampire, tall and pale-faced, hair black and descending to a widow's peak, fake fangs protruding from his mouth. Red makeup drips from the corners of his lips.

"I believe this is a time when the spirits come out of their hiding places," Daniel says, staring straight into the camera.

"Oh, the veil wears thin, that kind of thing?" Yolanda asks.

"They crawl out of attics, closet doors left ajar, basement portals unsecured," Daniel says.

Johnny, dressed as a big tube of toothpaste, nods sagely.

"I blame climate change," he says.

IRENE AND JEN BROWN
TEACHERS

A pair of mummies, meticulously wrapped up in coffee-stained bandages, adorned in the golden jewelry of ancient Egyptian queens.

"What do you make of the graves appearing in the street here?"

Irene, whose crown glitters with jade jewels, shakes her head.

"I think those religious sickos putting on the Trunk or Treat are behind it," she says. "Give themselves something to crow about, to prove that people who like Halloween are all sickos and freaks."

Jen nods, a large black crocheted spider bobbing on her shoulder as she does so.

"We're good, honest people," she says. "Just because we like Halloween doesn't mean we're evil, or that we would endorse all this." She gestures at the street.

"What *is* all this, do you think?" Salazar asks.

"This nation was formed and perpetuated by a death cult," Jen says. "The whole country is one big Indian burial ground, to namecheck a problematic trope. Of course things like this will happen from time to time."

"It's a wonder the whole country isn't going full-on *Poltergeist* all the time," Irene says.

"You think this phenomenon says something about the state of the nation?"

"Everything just gets worse," Irene says.

"Everything just gets worse," Jen echoes, her yarn spider nodding in assent.

Salazar turns to the camera, eager to be done with the interviews.

"No one has an explanation for the emergence of these graves and tombs on Main Street," she says. "But it's Halloween, and spirits remain high. Most locals remain weirdly calm about the entire situation."

A gaggle of costumed children rush by, laughing and tripping over their own feet.

"The children are certainly unfazed. For Channel 3 News, reporting from Canaltown, I'm Yolanda Salazar."

Gravedirt

ne, six, alpha, bravo, five, beta, three, two, two. One, six, alpha, bravo, five, beta, three, two, two—return to that darker, unmaintained, forgotten corner of the cemetery set among tilted trees and overgrown grass, where only the deer visit to hide from predators. On a low rise to the west, a set of headstones is arrayed in a semicircular clutch, a group of conspirators gathered in the protective shadows of the wood for malign purpose. These stones will constitute the first assembled elements of—surprise!—this film's slasher villain.

The strange stars above, visible through a break in the grey clouds, bear witness to Gravedirt's arrival. Dirt and pebbles levitate. Headstones shudder and crack. A low rumble rises from the soil, heralding the release of eldritch energies, until now ever-present but untapped.

From the worms and the wet earth, from granite chunks of grave marker and headstone, from the dry bones of the forgotten dead, Gravedirt is pulled together by psychic rivers of despair and anxiety. Can a collection of dirt, chunks of tombstones, metal marker plates, crumbling crypts, and human remains—formed into a hulking golem by psychospheric pressures—possess a shred of agency? Is the spiral of violence about to unfold an inevitability? Does this warrant a deep and meaningful explanation, or are such narratives perfunctory, mere rituals performed without enthusiasm or craftsmanship by hack horror writers since the 1980s?

Gravedirt is not alive in any sense that we might relate to, but is nonetheless able to exert *will*, either their own or that of the force that animates them. The killings will begin, soon.

The real question here, repeated early, often, and with growing worry, is: How did they pull off the special effect? CGI? Practical effects? Stop motion? Some inspired combination thereof?

Gravedirt's amalgam, Frankenstein-patchwork appearance is not only memorable and arresting in its visualization of cemetery debris taken human form— it looks *real*, shot in-camera. There is no zipper to be seen or obvious digital manipulation. There is only the stone, the dirt, the slabs of headstones and metal, the whorls of dust, the conflagration of bone, all assembled in humanoid form, moving heavy and deliberate, stalking through each shot with a physical *presence* that is both thrilling and worrisome. Watching Gravedirt stalk off through the trees has you caught between a nervous laugh and a desire to stop playback of the video.

It's not too late, you know. You can walk away whenever you want.

A short way through the trees to the south lies a house long abandoned. It once stood sentinel over a collection of short fields now grown fallow. The property was occupied and useful once, back when a person could make a living with a few dozen acres and the sweat of their brow, before the corporate farms and the chemicals that poisoned the soil and contaminated the neighbors' crops in exchange for a few good but short years of higher yields. Back when you could get lots of work hauling hay bales, feeding cows, and fixing fences, and you could buy a house for you and yours on the earnings, and not have to think too hard about the future.

This house will remain empty until it is dragged down to the soil by a conspiracy of time and gravity. Its doomed partner is a two-story barn, long and hollow, further along in its decline, beginning to tilt at strange angles, its support beams slipping out of place, its stone walls on the ground floor bulging, heralding collapse. Not even bored kids risk exploring its vermin-infested and scat-filled chambers. The barn and house are lonely in ways that only truly forgotten places can be, and so, when the swirling mass in human countenance of stone, soil, and bone that is Gravedirt emerges from the tree line to stalk heavily across the overgrown cornfields and yard, they are the first visitor on two legs in a generation. They move quietly, smoothly, surely, despite the odd contours of their patchwork body.

The barn is their destination—that symbol of agrarian labor, of struggle against the land itself, of sweat and blood and bloody colonization. The barn was church for those who placed their faith in *hard work* and *individual responsibility,* idols that made for poor, fickle gods as time marched on and the lords of this stolen New World sought cheaper labor and goods elsewhere.

Inside, the air is that of a tomb, moldy and thick with the miasma of piled-up bird and mouse excrement. There are dead animals here, too, having crawled in or been dragged here by their killers. The tractor is gone but its tires, bolts, metal bars, and the fuel tank remain, covered in rust. Tools, curiously, *conveniently* still sharp, hang from nails over troughs where cows once fed. Gravedirt makes a choice, then, their first real act of self-actualization, of self-definition, as everything leading up to this point had been decided for them, as is the way and tragedy of all things born into this world of horror.

Pitchfork, sledgehammer, shovel, or scythe?

Gravedirt choses the scythe. Their head—a whirling mass of broken grave marker chunks and the split half of a decrepit human skull—nods, satisfied, toward our POV.

Static and ghost-images overtake this shot of our killer-to-be in triumph. The synthesizer soundtrack swells, only to be replaced by the groaning notes of a church organ.

Ad Break from a Previous Recording Accidentally (?) Preserved on the Digital Rip of the VHS

Three coffins on a stage, set among flickering candelabras, grinning plastic skulls, and rolling fog. A burning-red candle. A grimoire of mystical power. Stock footage of a secluded German village, of trees in day-for-night. A figure in a purple robe and hood standing on a dark forest path. A laboratory of bubbling concoctions and ominous metal instruments. A necropolis dungeon, where the lantern-wielding living evade the grasps of the resurrected Templar dead. Faces in ghastly white makeup, with bright red blood dripping from their leering smiles, underlit by unflattering light.

Tune in for the horror event of the year, a voice says, masculine and deep but distorted and distant. A recording of a recording, complete with ambient electronic buzzing and, perhaps, the muffled voices of people whispering in a nearby room in the dead of night.

A vampiress with flowing red hair and a redder brooch, her white dress slashed with blood. Stained-glass Michael the Archangel putting the spear to a devil. Recorded-over afterimages of fire and panicked shadows, of a ghost in the tape, bag over its head, arms outstretched, beginning to levitate, seeking to escape the eternal recurrence of suffering.

The Crypt of Blood: A Halloween TV Special, the announcer says, this time with a bit of a rush to their delivery, an urgency that cuts through their old-style horror movie trailer cadence. *Performed by the Front Range Community Theater Troupe, based on the novel by Countess Blair Oscar Wilflame.*

Rubber bats on fishing wire, bobbing in the air. Robed figures standing in a circle in the woods, blood-red vampire eyes overlaid.

The words tumble out faster now, panic setting in, the words awkward and coughed out as a twisted, gleaming blade of occult provenance is pressed against their throat:

Generously sup-supported by—Malthus Corpse—Corporation, International—M-m-m-althus Arts and Sciences Philanth—

The knife's patience is exhausted. The announcer sputters out their last words, rushing to beat the rush of blood pouring from the fresh wound.

A Halloween TV...Special—G-Goatman...Secrets of the DEAD—

A castle stage set, burning. Ropes and curtains, cast and crew, aflame. Screaming.

Spook—show—

The presentation's title card glows royal purple, a wave of red blood hastily washing down the screen:

THE CRYPT OF BLOOD
A HALLOWEEN TV SPECIAL
AIRING OCTOBER 2007 –
FOREVERMORE

A Disquieting, Locally Produced Commercial for Robert "Rob" Cunningham and Cunningham Associates Realty Services

Clean, crisp interior of a whitewashed kitchen in a McMansion-style house, one of dozens built nearly identically to dozens more. Small kitchen island with faux-marble surface, set of four solid oak stools in attendance. New oven/microwave/refrigerator matching set in tasteful off-white, complete with Bluetooth connectivity and "smart" features to bombard marks with messages about overdue milk and egg purchases and software upgrades. Monthly subscription fees so low you won't even notice them, until you're a year into paying for a music app on an icemaker that doesn't even work. Everything can be *licensed*; nothing can be *owned*.

A smiling man and woman—the couple—run their hands over the island and the countertops, examining the tastefully placed track lighting that spits out harsh white illumination from above.

"Let's put in a bid," Gil, just north of 40, tall and

handsome, but with an off-putting intensity in his blue-grey eyes, says to Hannah, just north of 30, pretty but with rings under her eyes from overwork at her *very-much-back-to-the-office* job in downtown Rochester where she helps regional corporate executives make PowerPoint presentations to justify their annual bonuses.

Dark outside, ominous—a low dolly-in shot of the kitchen's main window, the focus beyond the glass to the expansive yard that runs into those of the clone houses beyond. Glittering eyes swell open, a low thrum of bass rising to distortion. It's late in the day to be looking at houses. But the market, being what it is, necessitates sacrifice and draws out the stink of desperation in everyone, including a happy, healthy, well-off, and spiritually deadened white couple like Gil and Hannah.

Close-up of Hannah smiling, her wide eyes catching the harsh light from above, her hands nervously running over the gas knobs on the stove, playacting letting them run, letting them *fill up the whole goddamn house.* She nods, imagining a future here, and half-imagining a gruesome end to that possibility, the smile on her face wicked but genuine. Gil misinterprets that semi-erotic excitement for anticipation of a life they might build here, together, and almost feels the love for her that he felt when they started dating, five years ago. Almost.

Hannah turns toward Geoff, the real estate agent—a third awkward figure in the kitchen, standing at the center of the room, rubbing the sweat from his bald head despite the chill of the late hour. The lights dim suddenly, the wind swelling up against the house, the eyes outside in the dark blinking shut. He reaches up to tap at one of the bulbs cupped in plastic set in an overhead track. His finger makes an unpleasant, sizzling-rapping sound against the cheap glass.

"We're going to make an offer," Hannah says.

The agent stares into the dying light, unblinking. Gil places a hand on the island countertop that separates him from his wife.

"Oh, this house?" Geoff says several beats too slow, his voice amplified by the bare walls of the kitchen to an uncomfortable degree.

"Yes, we like the house, and the location would be great for—"

"No, you wouldn't like *this* house, ma'am. No, not at all." The lights dim again for a longer, more uncomfortable interval, only to return brighter than before, casting a gruesome pallor over Geoff's face. He mumbles and whispers, his lips failing to form sentences coherently. Then, having gathered himself:

"This house has *bugs*."

He points toward the ceiling, which, just moments before, had been high and painted eggshell white, home to a skylight. Now, it is lower somehow, sealed off and full of crawling shadows.

"You know what I mean by 'bugs,' don't you?" Geoff brings his finger back down to his lips, signaling quiet. "*Someone is listening in, even now,*" he whispers, so low it can barely be heard over a bass line thrum that menaces the audio track. "Someone can hear us. Someone can *see* us. Someone can know our thoughts."

"I don't understand," Gil says, smiling, bright. It's

a winning smile, or should be, but is powerless here. "Should we come back tomorrow? I know we probably can't put the offer in until then anyway, but we want to make sure that..."

The agent shakes his head.

"I don't know how long this will last," Geoff says, eyes bulging from their sockets, fresh sweat bursting from the pores of his brow and streaming down his reddened face. "But now, *right* now, this house is infested. *Haunted.* And whatever is here, with us, will be with us, at least until..." His eyes flick toward the camera's POV—to you—for the slimmest of moments, with the briefest register of recognition and horror: the realization that the artifice of his present circumstances—and, perhaps, his entire existence—is becoming unwound.

A flash of color bars and austere tone, then a clumsily assembled, low-resolution placard of the improperly upscaled, pixelated logo of **Robert "Rob" Cunningham and Cunningham Associates Realty Services** and attendant smiling, bloated faces of Rob himself, his cursed offspring, and various hangers-on staring out into the oblivion of local broadcast television signal reach. Their skin is waxen, their eyes dull, their tears of blood trailing down their frozen faces in the slim moments before the color bars and tone reemerge to consume them, to snap the signal, to tear a bleeding fissure in perception and, therefore, the world itself.

The Charred Man

The covered bridge sags over a lustrous stretch of flowing creek water, its angular roof kissed by bright red leaves. Golden-hour sunlight reaches out over the distant hills to warm Hayden and Fiona's faces. The bridge becomes a shadow framed in amber.

Hayden leads Fiona up the forest path toward the bridge. She's ten now, just on the edge of giving up this trick-or-treating thing for good, and he's fifteen, half a lifetime older. She stopped holding his hand—rather, he stopped *letting* her hold his hand—years ago, so when she reaches for him and her cold fingers grasp his, he is caught off guard.

"We can't cross that way," Fiona says, her voice muffled behind the plastic green glow-in-the-dark skeleton mask. The eyes are holographic, reflecting multicolored skulls that shift and change depending on Hayden's vantage point. He searches for his own face in those eyes, but he finds only death.

Frustration heats up inside him. He didn't even want to be taking her out tonight. He had better things to do—well, that's what he told their parents, anyway—than taking his weird little sister out to get candy on Halloween night. He even tried the "it's a school night" argument, a gambit so unexpected that his father laughed out loud when Hayden delivered it with an earnest face, as if studying and getting a good night's sleep were ever on the agenda for him. Now, not even twenty minutes from stepping out the front door, her bag barely containing any candy after only a couple of stops, she was arguing with him. Typical.

He pulls his hand away.

"We cross the creek here, follow the canal up a ways, and we'll be in one of those McMansion neighborhoods," he says, trying not to scold her, but knowing he sounds condescending all the same. His father's voice his own, despite his best efforts. A preview of things to come. "They got the full-size candy bars over there."

"You don't know that," Fiona says, shifting on her feet, her polyester Grim Reaper's cloak shuffling. "Rich people aren't generous. It's the friendly retired people and the day-drinking suburban parent types who give out the good stuff. We can't go that way, anyway." She lifts her plastic scythe to point its curved blade north. "The bridge is out."

Hayden frowns, then looks to the bridge. The afterburn of the descending sun is gone, and his eyes—in handheld, DSLR POV—auto-adjust to the dark and shadow, revealing the footbridge stuffed full of strange shapes and menacing shadows.

"Don't," Fiona says, concern in her voice, but Hayden is already off, hands stuffed in his hoodie pocket, regretting not wearing his winter coat, his sneakers crunching against the overgrown gravel laid over the municipal forest trail that leads up to the bridge. The water flows orange and yellow and black in the fading light, and the air is the freshest and sharpest he has ever breathed. He reaches the edge of the bridge's crooked panels embedded in the dirt, and the stink of freshly upturned earth overwhelms his nose.

At first, the obstruction appears as great, flat shapes, all piled together. Maybe the trail people closed off the bridge for repairs. After all, the bridge was old—old enough to have been a spot where his mom and her high school friends used to come hang out, just like the kids do these days—and it needs some love and care every few years to keep it from collapsing into the water. But the earthy smell is distinct from the mud of the creek bed below. The shapes are at odds with the context of the bridge and the creek, objects at war with their placement, scrambling Hayden's understanding of his own perception. Fiona joins him at the precipice, pausing before she takes a tentative step out onto the bridge. Where her brother froze, uncomprehending, she is drawn to the impossibilities.

A flashlight beam clicks on, spearing the air between them, pooling across the grave markers, the clumsily piled soil, the weeping angels, the Mothers Mary, the redeemed Christs, the stones with names and date ranges and citations of wartime military service, of *loving mothers* and *beloved children* and so much more, impossibly crammed into the footbridge over a minor creek running parallel to the Erie Canal.

Hayden and Fiona turn around to find the source of the light. Framed between them stands a short but older-than-Hayden girl, her oversized, patch-covered jean jacket hanging off her like a burial shroud. In her right hand she holds the flashlight, which she sweeps up to their faces quickly and back down again, just long enough to get a look at them. A white cylinder trails smoke upward from her left hand, which she brings up to her lips for a quick pull.

Hayden recognizes her, or thinks he does, recalling her long black hair and her pretty face that's one of so many that haunt him in the hallways of Canaltown High School. She is older and has a bad reputation, as pretty older girls often do, and is thus of another world: lovely and dangerous in his mind, in the simple and selfish way that young boys think. He is suddenly embarrassed to be here, trick-or-treating with his younger sister, and his stomach clenches with a sense of vulnerability, of pending mockery, from this girl or from others who might be with her. He will be haunted by many such self-obsessed but no less terrifying phantasms in the difficult years ahead.

"If you think *that's* wild, check *this* shit out," the older girl says, blowing out smoke that lingers in the air with an unfamiliar but not unpleasant smell. She angles the light to a spot beside the bridge, letting it lead her—and them, wary but willing to follow—to where the earth curls back and falls away to the creek a dozen feet below. The three of them walk over to the edge, looking down into the abyss.

A conflagration of stone and wooden caskets, broken and misaligned statuary, stretches of stained glass, and stone staircases poke up out of the water. There are no bodies—just carved skulls and craven gargoyles of stone and alabaster, mischievous moss-covered devils clinging to dislodged ossuary roofs, the impassive faces of solemn angels. A sedimentary layer of the grave.

"What is it?" Fiona asks. Curious, not scared.

"Nobody knows," Hayden says.

"Bullshit," the girl says, blowing out more smoke. "Somebody knows."

"What do *you* think it is?" Hayden asks, hoping his voice doesn't slip or crack or his words get tangled on their way out. She shrugs.

"The end, probably. If not for everything, then for us, eventually." The older girl pauses for emphasis. "Anyway, she's right, I wouldn't try to cross through *that* for any amount of candy. You'd be wasting your time, anyway. The development along the canal on the far side isn't good for trick-or-treating. Bunch of Boomer-brained reactionaries with their porch lights off, 'Jesus Saves' in their front yards for the Halloween season. Real pricks."

"What are 'reactionaries'?" Hayden says.

"What's your name?" Fiona asks. "You go to Canaltown, right?" The girl gives Fiona a bright, sincere smile.

"Anna. You?"

"Fiona."

"You're the specter of Death, Fiona."

"Yes. Most people just think I'm a skeleton."

"Close enough. Do you know what a memento mori is, Fiona?"

"Yes."

"I'm Hayden," he says, awkward, cutting in, not wanting to be left out. *Shit. Don't sound so stupid.*

Anna gives him a big wink.

"Hi, big guy." As if remembering her manners, she holds out the joint. "Smoke?"

"Yes! I mean, no, sorry. I'm supposed to—taking care of—we need to..."

"It's cool," Anna says, giving him an amused smile. "Those are my friends over there." She angles her head back over her shoulder. A group of shadows stands at the edge of the trail on the far side, drawn-up hoodies and green glow sticks, smoke wafting up from them. Hayden's stomach clenches in fight-or-flight response. Waiting for the snickering, the insults, calling them any number of slurs, implying any number of deviant or non-normative sexual orientations, behaviors, identities.

Those types of interactions had gotten less frequent as he had grown older, a little bigger, and quicker to tighten his fists, to lift his gaze and raise his voice to the dipshits who might throw those words his way.

He still feels flashes of those vulnerabilities, those sore spots made permanent, dug out at first not by kids at school or on the street but by his own family—those parents and aunts and uncles who taunted him, mocked him for crying when he was too young to know his own age, teasing him about how he looked, constantly talking about the bodies of women or the sexual preferences of other men, mocking the cartoons or movies he liked, putting down the interest he showed in anything besides cars, hunting, or sports.

But that is the past, he reminds himself. He lets it all go with a wave of his hand and a nod of acknowledgment to the shadows beyond the edge of the trail. Despite being immersed in the manias of young adulthood, he is already building the resiliency that will see him grow up into someone Not So Bad—assuming he survives the horrors to come in this digital video nightmare.

"The dead are always with us," Anna says through a haze of smoke, smoke so thick it's a rolling fog rising up from the creek. Hayden and Fiona realize that's not a cigarette Anna's smoking, and they wonder about the possibility of a contact buzz—a get-out-of-jail free card for mind alteration, with enough plausible deniability for others and, more importantly, their own consciences, which have been warped by the War on Drugs mentality of the adults in their lives. "Especially on Halloween. We'll join them soon."

"I'm not in a hurry," Fiona says.

"Life's short," Anna says, shrugging, affecting a beyond-her-years wisdom. Pretending to know or understand profound truths of the world is easy when you're young.

The shadows step forward, faces revealed in the pink and gold light of sunset, half-imbibed light beers and wine coolers and clove cigarettes in their hands. Fog/smoke permeates the trail, heavy and unrelenting. Fiona smells ozone and upturned earth. Anna is just about to introduce her friends when a reverberation cuts through the atmosphere like a biblical herald, charged with static and terror.

Life is a dream, a projection in your mind, the mind a screen, your perceptions a camera generating a simulacrum of reality, it says, with all of the hurried, awkward syllabic cadence of an amateur actor, stoned out of his mind, reciting his lines through a cheap microphone for ADR. The voice redlines and is laden with post-processing effects that draw the words out into unnerving configurations—or perhaps the recording has been exposed to heat, and is thus warped and malign. *Reality would be otherwise impossible, and is made manifest solely through the interactions of transmission and reception. The observer strives to become the observed and back again. In such a way as to guarantee that none can ever be truly alone. Not even God.*

Anna isn't screaming, not exactly. Her friends are rushing toward her, Hayden, and Fiona, having spied the creature in the wood line first and eager to put distance between them. Anna is trying to translate her terror into actionable words, but the interface of mind, tongue, mouth, throat, lungs, and so on fails her, and she is instead shocked into spasmatic moaning. What she sees—like Hayden first encountering the cemetery debris on the bridge— short-circuits those interrelated systems of synthesis of perception, understanding, and communication.

Purple eyes vomit up illumination from a depth of deep black, overlaid with stringy red slime and flesh hanging on a vaguely humanoid form. Its arms are raised, stuntman-in-a-monster-suit style, waddling awkwardly toward them.

Your understanding is not required for process to occur. Essential symmetries continue to form and un-form. Schism and imbalance perpetrated by human maladaptation can only be tolerated by a system desiring equilibrium for so long.

Harbingers of restoration appear as fearsome as the surgeon's gleaming saw and scalpel to the infected flesh, from which pain, death, and disease might be drawn out.

Fiona's hand is in Hayden's once more, and they are the first to run back down the trail, back toward town. Anna and the others are moving now, too, but Anna hesitates, not out of some failure of self-preservation, but out of naked curiosity. Recognizing this, the Charred Man halts his lumbering advance in the middle of the path, smoke rising from his dumpy, rounded head, shoulders, and floppy, rubbery arms, which he points at her in acknowledgment.

A wonder for the wonderless, wondrous for observer-observed. Remember this encounter of intelligences.

For Anna, alone now—the others bounding down the trails maintained by the good senior citizen volunteers of the Canaltown Hiking and Trails Committee—the sky becomes a film negative, the trees are reduced to ashen cinders, the leaves and grass vaporize, and the bridge is blown apart by a demon wind. In its place, rising from the creek bed, is a stone monolith. The alternatingly smooth and geometrically complex structure stands tall, curving almost imperceptibly to a sharp point that pierces the sky. At its tip a collection of skeletal antennae glow with purple light in imitation of a cell-phone or radio-broadcast tower.

The Charred Man reaches for her—for *us*, in POV—in a jump cut so sudden that its intended effect as a jump scare is elevated by the amateurishness of its desynchronization with the soundtrack.

Anna—we—see stock footage wonders. The birth of a cow in a dingy, underlit barn, pulled out of her mother by men covered in the gore of life; the burning-death of great mountain forests; the serial numbers of American-made bombs melting away as they impact schools and hospitals; the first shared look of two people who will grow to love one another truly and fully until death; the whispered footsteps of a ghost hovering over well-worn floorboards in a haunted house.

Sensing confusion, the Charred Man releases his psychic grip on her (your/our) mind.

Practical demonstration of component concept in lieu of totality of understanding—

Anna stumbles back a step as the Charred Man, now within reach, holds his arms out in crucifix stance, glitching out into a T-pose, throwing his round head back to stare at the sky. His melting lips open wide, trailing flesh, to reveal the emerging cap of a full-sized human skeleton. Blackened teeth break and flick off like popcorn kernels jumping in a pan of hot oil. The charred flesh-slime sloughs off in stinking curtains of rot, and the emerging skeleton form is screaming, Anna is *screaming*, and the world flashes between quantum states, one or zero, on or off, active or inactive, until the difference between the living and the dead is understood as illusion, an affectation for dramatic effect, no more real or less real than a special effect in a DIY horror movie nightmare.

Vampire Castle Arcade

On a stretch of Elm Street—because every town needs an Elm Street in October—slicing southwards off of Main, there runs a length of brick commercial buildings constructed at the tail end of the 1880s, back when the Erie Canal still vainly competed with rail. They are grey, red, and brown brick, with hand-carved ornamental features upon layered outcroppings, windowsills, and arched doorways. Well maintained over the following century and a half, these remnants of Canaltown's once-robust downtown are a link to local and regional history—and living reminders of a glorious past, weighted and ornamented with nobility and simple but evocative design.

To emphasize Elm Street's out-of-time psychogeography, the businesses in these brick temples have miraculously survived decades of austerity neoliberalism, rural disinvestment, a global pandemic, health care deserts, and the ongoing pharmaceutical company–driven opioid and fentanyl crises. Among these survivors is the Vampire Castle Arcade. Eschewing the insufferable trend toward cynical alcohol-centric "barcades," this relatively small but vital feature of technological and artistic heritage has maintained a stable core of classic and new machines in a dingy, dark, and suitably dungeonesque interior mercifully free of sloppy, slack-mouthed drunks spilling disgusting IPAs onto studiously engineered and lovingly designed machines of great cultural value.

That is not to say that people don't drink at the Vampire Castle Arcade. Altered states of consciousness are quite acceptable here, within reason. A tastefully hidden flask, a Coke can spiked with cheap vodka, or a pre-game of a few beers before the visit helps many patrons experience the time distortion, blur, and haze of the interior of the Vampire Castle to a slightly more pronounced degree than normative states of consciousness.

The current owner—one of several in a long line of quiet, keep-to-themselves types who must have some other means of maintaining a living, because the Vampire Castle can't possibly be profitable enough to survive on its own, especially with rampant inflation driven by the bloodsucking bastards who control the US economy (the *real* vampires, amirite?)—might encourage other means of altering one's consciousness. She might recommend the low-grade acid sold by a man who calls himself "Hound Dog" and frequents the jam band shows held every summer down near Watkins Glen; the peyote grown on a distant reservation, which has a better-than-even chance of attracting the attention of Coyote Spirit, who is eager to lead you deep into the forest for a rendezvous with beings those of Irish heritage might recognize as the people of the fairy mounds; or simply cannabis, especially the strain imported from

Colorado and shared among the seekers and the isolated—the aforementioned King in Yellow, whose blue and amber veins and crystals can produce a special resonance field within the foggy, dark, and electronic noise-ridden atmosphere of the Vampire Castle.

It is this latter strain that you have imbibed before...before...(*watching the film? entering the arcade? reading this book? All three?*)...sneaking a quick inhale or two via a one-hitter pipe. A couple of puffs is all you will need to experience the arcade at maximum transcendental power.

The wide windows of the brick building's exterior are decorated with paper skeletons dancing, vampires snarling, and mummies lumbering, all composed in an exaggerated cartoon style on thin card-paper cutouts. Black rubber bats swarm the entrance, hanging along fishing wire from the overhang. The glass door itself is framed by the sharp teeth of a ravenous jack o'lantern, the entryway threatening to consume those who enter, including, now, you (or the camera's POV).

The interior is dim and the ceiling hangs low, reflecting the soft light of arcade cabinet screens and bulbous CRTs that shed a dizzying array of color and movement. The ether is alive with a tangle of competing melodies, crunchy sound effects, and digitized voices. The attract modes running all at once at different lengths and rhythms are overstimulating, especially as the first real effects of the King's touch are felt across your nervous system. The overload becomes pleasant, however, as the noise and music produced by ancient sound chips using analog logic, mechanical trickery, and primitive digital samples flood over you in a wave of entrancing nostalgia, calling back to a time when video game experiences were works of magic that could pull you out of the mundane drudgery and constant anxiety of your childhood.

Overwhelmed by sound, dark, and intermittent light, your mind is temporarily free of its present neuroses—its deep, recurring shames, its pathetic patterns of self-hate, and its unresolved worries about the rapidly collapsing future over which you, as an individual, can exercise no control at all.

The ghoul who mans the counter gives you a lipless smile. His face is decay, his one remaining eyeball dripping out of a black socket, patches of hair stubbornly clinging to his taut scalp. A soft, pained whistle can just be heard over the electronic din as he pretends to breathe through a naked nasal cavity. His uniform is impeccable: a black T-shirt with the faded image of Christopher Lee as Dracula reaching for a victim, eyes bloodshot and wide; sun-bleached jeans, ripped and loose; and a name tag perched over the spot where the ghoul's heart might be:

U.R. NECKS
Cabinet Maintenance & Senior Spookster

You put down a twenty-dollar bill and the creature hands you a sack of coins, his one remaining eye never bothering to count out the money, his lidless gaze unwavering. You nod and whisper *thanks* before heading past the glass cases full of scattered fun-size chocolate bars, candy corn, and pumpkins, plastic spider and skull rings, glow sticks, and more, and make for the nearest cluster of cabinets. As you approach, the dark shroud that hangs over everything—making it all unreal and distant, like film-negative fog—suddenly lifts, allowing you to see through the murk to the distinct cabinet artwork of heroes, villains, musclemen, warrior women in armor, and gruesome bio-horrors; the glowing, more-vibrant-than-reality screens; the soft green lights running along the carpet in a crooked path through the arcade to guide pilgrims on their journey into a realm of technological sorcery and forgotten wonders.

You open the bag of tokens: thin but weighty metal with semi-sharp ridges that produce a satisfying sensation when you run your thumb over them. There's a skull in profile on one side, and on the other a jack o'lantern half-rotted, smiling back in raised relief. Unlimited free play just doesn't feel the same as having to pop in a coin for another go, even if those coins are cheap.

There are many machines here, and you have enough tokens to spend all of Halloween evening and night among them, with the ghoul at the front counter your only company. You feel his eye upon you, and you know that if you were to turn you would find him staring at you with something like hunger—like gleeful anticipation—radiating off of him in malignant psychic waves.

Your eyes sweep across the initial slate of arcade machines, passing by the more popular cabinets likely to draw in the normie arcade-curious crowds: classics like *Ms. Pac-Man, Dig Dug,* a *Nintendo PlayChoice-10,* and so on. Personal favorites like

Street Fighter III: Third Strike, Splatterhouse, Darkstalkers, and *Aliens* tempt you to stop and spend your tokens, but the parallel tracks of green mini bulbs encased in transparent plastic tubing along the benighted path wind on in a labyrinth of electronic delights. GO LEFT for *Area 51, House of the Dead 2*, and more light-gun games; GO RIGHT for *Salamander, R-Type Leo, Deathsmiles*, and an array of shoot-em-ups. The illuminated path directly before you invites you to GO STRAIGHT.

The open floor space grows expansive, the dark aglow with constellations of ambient purples, oranges, and greens stretching beyond what you assumed were the limits of the building itself. Blacklights illuminate the mallwave pattern of the carpet and velvet blood-red texture of the walls.

You find a stone archway at the end of the green bulb trail. "The Gaming Graveyard" is announced by hand-painted, blood-red words on a plank of rotting wood suspended from the ceiling before the entrance to a ring of stone wall and cemetery fencing that encircles the inmost den. The fence's metal bars are interwoven with pulsing vines of malignant green and flowers of robust purple and gold. Shadows scurry and shift on the dark ceiling above. The air smells of earth freshly disturbed for an imminent burial or three.

You step beneath the archway. There is a ring of arcade machines here. There are other patrons hunched over the machines of this special cloister, their faces fleshless or otherwise decaying and aglow with the light of screens bulging with digital horrors.

Choosing which machine to start with is difficult.

At first, you are drawn to the melancholy Gothic adventure of *The Drunkard's Dream*, but having spent a couple of summers playing that at a small arcade on a family trip to the great and distant mountains you are content to let that game and its colorful denizens live within your memories. You move on.

Dr. Coagulant's Splatter Lab calls to you, and this is where you spend your first half-dozen tokens. It is a top-down *Gauntlet* clone with horror trappings, bigger sprites, less quarter-munching cruelty, and gruesomely explicit monster death animations. You play a mutated hero bound to a spiritual parasite—a talking chainsaw—that grants him the power to rip enemy monsters and biofreaks limb from slime-covered limb. You fight zombies across the toxic wasteland of a post–ghost apocalypse landscape, then battle mutoids and a vine-plant monster in an abandoned high school. A dark and ominously empty tunnel leads you to the splatter labs of Dr. Coagulant himself, where the constant barrage of attacks from the boss-rush endgame consumes both your patience and your tokens.

Each time you die, your avatar wakes up in a coffin in a shallow grave, not far from where the action ended. The screen is mostly black, with just a few slashes of moonlight shining through layers of hastily dumped sediment and an ooze-green "CONTINUE...?" prompt. After you drop in more tokens, you must bash the attack button to punch your way up and out of the coffin and dig yourself back to the surface. It takes more and more effort each time, increasing the tension with every death.

As fatigue sets in and you fail to defeat the final boss on your latest attempt, you allow the darkness of the grave to swallow you whole. The GAME OVER notification slides down the screen in a flood of purple slime. The spiritual parasite's laughter echoes from hidden speakers, audible even as you move on to the next machine.

Skeleton Demesne is not explicitly horror, but its atmosphere and themes are suitable for Halloween. You assume the role of Skeleton Lord, a lich who must defend his subterranean crypt from waves of crusading adventurers. With limited time and a somewhat awkward control scheme of joystick and three buttons—and a series of brief instruction screens played during attract mode—you set up traps and place monsters across an isometric, early 3D polygon dungeon landscape.

Skeleton warriors are cheap and have a chance to resurrect when killed, and make good fodder to slow down the advancing waves of would-be tomb raiders. Goblin archers are slow but their flaming arrows pierce armor and cause ongoing damage via the burn condition. Maulotaurs can charge and smash into hapless adventurers, sending them flying with great swings of their wrecking balls or goring them to death on their massive horns. Mummies are expensive units, but they can grab greedy heroes looking for jewels in coffins and sarcophagi for insta-kills. Pendulum blades, hidden spike pits, murder holes, and fire-spraying stone dragon heads all provide creative and colorful deaths for the AI opponents, who are relentless in their meatgrinder march into your dungeon.

But your resources are limited, and your legion of reanimated corpses is not inexhaustible. The colonizers simply just keeping coming and, lacking a metastrategy to stem the flow of paladins, clerics, swordmen, dwarven axe fighters, barbarians, and crossbow-wielding rogues, you are eventually overwhelmed. You are not sure if there is a true win state for the machine, or if a high score is the best you can ever hope for.

ClownEvil is next, enticing you with a first-person light-gun experience of candy colored carnage, of grim calliope music radiating from blown-out speakers. Inserting a few of your rapidly diminishing tokens yields a cutscene where you find a clown mask in a disintegrating cardboard box and slip it over your face. You can almost smell the cheap rubber and feel the condensation build against your skin. Your first-person view takes you down dilapidated exurban streets, where you fire a confetti gun at feral dogs, blast out windows to terrorize your digital neighbors, and set fire to police cars for major point multipliers.

With only a few tokens left, you become aware of a gathering around a nearby machine. The cabinet art is lurid, bloody, and sexually suggestive: a humanoid fish creature chasing a half-naked dude and babe across a beach, their swimwear shredded; a werewolf with unconscious victim clutched in its ravenous embrace; a vampiress in revealing corset and black cape gesturing for you to accept her bloody kiss; a miasma of a leering spirit gripping a screaming victim by her bare leg. Horror movie sound effects ring out from the cabinet: slices, dices, the wet impact of bodies, the digitized taunts of the monster-fighters as they tear each other apart.

White-sheet ghosts and decaying zombies crowd around the *Crypt Fighters* cabinet, their empty eye sockets trained on the dazzling images on the screen. A moan rises up from the murder of horrors, and one of the two players at the sticks and buttons steps away in defeat. There is a cloud of sulfurous smoke, the flapping of bat wings, and she is gone. None of the others step forward to take her place.

Leaning over the Player 2 position is a short figure wrapped in yellowed bandages wearing a crown and necklace of glittering blue jewels fitted into golden scarabs. This mummified princess turns her desiccated head, almost imperceptibly, to gesture for you to take your place at her side. The ghosts and ghouls, sensing the royal summons, shuffle aside to let you pass.

You plink a token into the *Crypt Fighters* slot and wrap your hands around the joystick. You piano your fingers across the buttons for various punches, kicks, and specials. You remember a few basic moves from this game, or others like it. Muscle memory.

The character selection screen screams into place, the bass-pumping Gothic electronica music keeping your focus and making your head bob involuntarily. Charming pixel-art portraits of the monsters you have known and loved all your life beckon to you, inviting you to choose, to become. The emaciated skeleton. The venerable mummy. The sexy demon. The hideous cryptmaster. The alluring vampire. The muscular mushroom-man. The ripped werewolf. The melting zombie. The ominous golem. The leering goblin. And more.

Choose your monster. Choose your idealized self as manifested through a prism of undeath and repressed desires. See in this fantasy world of violence and suggestive pixel art a glimmer of power, of self-actualization. Disappoint your parents and the local pastor. Enjoy the art and music and titillating animation. Do something pointless for a few rounds of fast-paced, classic monster combat. Play the game, get good at it, because it feels good, because this game of undeath lets you forget life for a little while.

The camera dollies backwards, away from the crowded cabinet. You see yourself leaning forward in anticipation of the contest. The dead watch, too. Fogs rolls in, subsuming all. The frame is aglow with soft, pleasant, electronic light.

Cartomancy Precedes the Carnival of Blood

Establishing shots and scattershot coverage of the Trunk or Treat Carnival in the municipal library parking lot: kids in costumes, dead-eyed parents drinking overpriced IPAs from small plastic cups, bored teenagers running games of chance with cheap stuffed animals for prizes. Police cars with their lights ablaze; volunteer firefighters handing out candy from plastic fire helmets. The sky is dark now, but the yellow, hazy light from the parking lot lamps and orange string lights refract off the camera lens and cast everything in muted amber.

Hayden and Fiona stumble out of the brush at the edge of the railroad tracks bisecting town. They are across the street from the library parking lot, weaving through parked cars to reach the festival. They fall in line with the gaggle of kids and adults waiting to pass through the entrance checkpoint. A pair of overweight men pat down the children in costumes and wave a metal detector wand over agitated parents. Security theater for the terminally disinterested and compliant.

Hayden glances back across the street, beyond

the railroad tracks. Here, the light makes everything in the distance fuzzy and indistinct. He strains his eyes, looking for the Charred Man, but that phantasm refuses to appear. He looks for Anna and her friends, too, but they are nowhere.

Strange, sweaty hands pass over them, and then they are moving through orange road cones and past metal folding chairs to enter the embrace of the crowd at the Trunk or Treat Carnival. Surrounded by their dead-eyed neighbors, the air awash in too-loud rhythms of the worst pop-country music imaginable, Hayden and Fiona do not quite relax—but the unreality of their present circumstances allows them to process the rupture to which they were both witness.

"Was he sick?" Fiona asks. "Did he need our help?"

"It was a costume," Hayden says, trying to convince himself. A child dressed as a bright red devil scampers by, disappearing in a press of high school kids who smell like weed and Miller Light.

"It wasn't," Fiona says. She shakes her head, trying to clear it, but that is impossible here. "Come on." She heads off toward the row of vendor tents at the far side of the library.

They snake through the crowd, bodies bumping against bodies, avoiding sloshing beer and scampering children. Realtor Robert "Rob" Cunningham and Cunningham Associates' large popup tent is abandoned. Just a folding card table with some pamphlets and business cards flanked by discarded red plastic cups. They pause here, in a break in the crowd.

"Should we tell someone? Mom and Dad?" Fiona asks.

"Tell them what?" Hayden counters, looking at his sister's face for the first time since their flight from the bridge. His own face softens when he sees the tears gathered around the edges of her eyes. "We're okay. I don't know what that was. But we're safe here."

"No, you're not," a voice says from within the next tent over. Irish lilt, but with some of the charming edges sanded off after years spent stateside. "None of us are. Not here."

Fiona's eyes go wide. Hayden puts a finger to his lips, then shuffles to the edge of the tent and angles his head around the side. Just a few feet over stands the next tent, this one made of cloth instead of plastic sheeting. Elaborately woven, colorful designs spread across coarse material, dark and inviting. Exuberant gold and jewels glint atop the headpiece and necklaces worn by the woman inside. Hayden gasps as her fire-red eyes catch his. Her long black hair is so dark that it glows. Red lips and pale skin are accentuated by shadow and bauble made inviting and mysterious by candlelight.

"The creature is not in pursuit, but another is coming," the woman says, her voice low and soft as Irish cream but perfectly audible all the same. "We have time to read the cards before the conflagration."

The wind is perfumed with cinnamon and sand. Hayden is pulled into the fortune teller's tent, drawn by curiosity and a sensation of desire like the fluttering of a bat's wings, his misgivings forgotten.

Fiona stumbles in after him, caught off guard by the finery within.

Shadows recede as they cross the threshold into the tent, revealing stacks of grimoires and scrolls of parchment laced with dust. Low-burning candles flicker from atop silver plates that amplify the light in strange patterns as they run heavy with melted wax. Rolled rugs, small displays of ornate, asymmetrical jewelry pieces, and hand-painted eye, human heart, and bat charms draw their attention and paw at their innate desires. Whispers of many voices flutter around them, hiding in the many-faceted flickering dark that lingers behind the woman.

She is beautiful, deep into middle age, her red eyes accentuated by pointed liner, her dark hair revealing itself to contain a menagerie of dyed colors, held in place by a veil that reaches down across her forehead. Her robe is of deepest black, inlaid with gold and shining red threads, evoking cosmological formation and connection in subtle patterns that are alive with strange fire.

Hayden and Fiona are seated before her, a small table covered in smooth green felt between them. The Tarot cards appear in the woman's hands in close-up, conjured by a spirit of the air.

"A dual reading for those whose fate is bound together, on this most auspicious of days," the woman says. The cards are the length and width of extended hands, overlarge and dancing between her ring-bound fingers. "A day fraught with signs and symbols, when the signifier and the signified collide, and become one and the same." She graces Hayden with a well-practiced and flirtatious smile. He blushes, despite himself. The smile she gives Fiona is softer, kinder, perhaps motherly. The girl feels the practiced warmth of that look in her core. The woman knows how to work her audience.

"There is a question of my fee."

"We don't have any money," Hayden says, ashamed and embarrassed, as if he has let her down.

The woman raises her eyebrows and curls her lower lip inward, as if thinking of a compromise. She turns her attention to Fiona.

"What is in your bag, young lady?"

"Um. Halloween candy."

"What kind of candy?"

Fiona's brow furrows. She reaches inside her bag, holding it wide open to let in splashes of candlelight.

"Licorice, chocolate bars, some of those sour candies."

"Do you have a Kotto Bar?"

"A what?"

"Locally produced candy. I knew its namesake, once. Our paths crossed when he consulted the Tarot on a case of his, involving a group of blood-stealing psychos in a medical van."

"Uh."

"I will read the Tarot for one Kotto Bar. Any size. It holds some sentimental value for me, even if it is not particularly good."

Fiona reaches in, shuffles around, and pulls out her prize: a half-sized candy bar in a plastic wrapper of road-cone orange, depicting a frowning man wearing a jet-black Stetson hat and too-large aviator sunglasses with a cigarette hanging out of his mouth. *KOTTO BAR*, it reads, in font almost too small.

PROCEEDS BENEFIT RE-ELECTION CAMPAIGN OF SHERIFF KOTTO. She does not recall which house she got this from, nor does she remember ever seeing it before. She hands it across the table to the fortune teller, turning it over in her fingers as she does so, revealing another caption: *ALL SPACE VAMPIRES ARE BASTARDS.* Fiona smiles at that phrase, finding it funny, even if she is not sure why.

The woman smiles as she passes her hand over Fiona's and the strange candy bar disappears. Then she is shuffling the cards again.

"The Tarot does not conjure devils or spirits. Its occult origins are overblown, but like all tools of divination, it contains no power on its own but merely acts as a focal point for the mind and spirit." She lays four of the oversized cards on the table before them, face down. "I will read two cards for each of you, whose fates are intertwined on this night of goblinry and darkness, four altogether, revealing one story."

She turns the first card to reveal an intricate illustration of a young boy and a young girl, standing upon a forest path, swords and shields in their hands. The prop is well lit from above, accentuating the colorful details of the image. Someone spent a lot of time on these designs. "Strength. Although you may often be at odds as siblings are, your lives are connected, and will remain so. The path you walk, you walk together, and your strength flows one to the other."

Hayden frowns at this. Fiona groans. The woman laughs, breaking her performance for a moment.

"You should treasure the connection you share.

Not all siblings get along—or can even be said to share a true familial love and bond. Rely upon one another in the hours ahead, and, if you survive, remember that strength is as a mirror catching light, illuminating a dark room."

She turns the second card. A skeleton, wielding a scythe, stands among downed bodies in a field of wheat. Fiona gasps.

"Death," the fortune teller says, almost a whisper. "Death does not mean you will die, but it does mean that change is imminent, that conflict—and resolution—are on the horizon." She smiles warmly at them both. "Do not fear—at least, not in this present moment. Let us interpret the pattern, the shape of the whole, and not from a place of superstition or fear." She turns the third card over.

A leering vampire, tall and stately in a purple cape, red eyes aglow and red fangs bared. He stands atop a castle battlement, blood dripping from his pale lips.

"The Hermit. Confrontation, with the threat of death—and change," she says. "A teacher can be seen as a threat—and, in some ways, *is*—but also offers a path to a new way of understanding. Whether you understand the lesson or not, and whether you survive the education, well..."

Against the card she taps a black fingernail with an eye painted in white that stares dumbly outward from its center. "We are surrounded by people, by community, such as it is, but some lessons are best learned in the wilderness, in the wasteland. In the dark." Her fingers flutter as she moves to the final card, and the painted-on eye shifts to another finger, and another, until it is gone. Her shadow, given free rein in the chaotic light of the reflected and refracted candles, flips the final card.

The card's face is revealed as a grey cassette with a crooked label: *Spooky Sounds from a Haunted House.*

"One last Halloween treat," the fortune teller says. "Play it when it is most needed." Her shadow's fingers slide beneath the cassette, pulling it from the card, making it three-dimensional and real.

Fiona leans back as the woman offers her the tape, but the fortune teller is patient, and her smile is warm. Fiona holds out her hand. The cassette is cool and lightweight in her palm. She drops it into her trick-or-treat bag.

Yelling from outside the tent draws their attention. A sudden draft of autumn cold snuffs out the candles.

"The reading is complete," the woman says, her voice an echo. The candles are reduced to wisps of smoke and globs of wax. A slouching beast of darkness crawls from the back of the tent to subsume the card reader, leaving only her red eyes visible and aglow. "I thank you for your patronage, and wish you luck on the benighted path ahead." Then her eyes disappear too, and there is a rustling of candy wrappers and fallen leaves.

The yelling outside the tent turns to screaming. Desperate voices, a rush of air, a change in the barometric pressure. The crowd, the collective animal-thing that it is, chooses panic. People rush by the tent, heavy feet slapping against the parking lot pavement.

All trace of the card reader is gone, as is the table, her jewelry stands, her books and scrolls, her dead candles. The tent's fabric blows upward and over them, sent flying into the air by the wind, collapsing into itself, compressing into whorls of blood-red leaves. The chairs become bones, rattling as they collapse. Hayden and Fiona stand up suddenly. The night air is sharp. The terrible music cuts out, replaced by screams.

Gravedirt, the living avatar of stone and death, wields their scythe with the practiced swing of a medieval peasant who lived a life of toil. Human heads roll off bodies, spraying blood in wide, wet arcs. Their torsos shudder, ejaculating the heart's last futile pumps from necks that look like crosscut bushels of sliced deli meat. Arms and hands reach out blindly, grasping like Frankenstein's monsters newly given life, before the headless bodies collapse to the hard pavement with wet *smacks*.

Crouching, robed figures flank the whirling stone and dirt and broken grave markers that form Gravedirt, that golem of destruction. From the folds of their grim brown and black-charred robes hands of bone emerge, wielding sickles, hammers, shovels, and short axes. These instruments of simple, deadly labor are sent forth to crush the skull plates of red-faced men in zombie makeup desperately clinging to their beers as they flee. A gaggle of middle-aged women in suggestive catgirl outfits are felled by axes with blades honed sharp, cut down like thin, sickly trees harvested for kindling. A group of teenaged boys dressed in some inexplicable homemade mishmash referencing a long-forgotten online meme-cultural moment are rushing to the perceived safety of the *just-too-far* parking lot when scythes and saws slice through the air (in rapid succession of blurry close-ups) to sever and saw necks, spilling blood and revealing the flesh and bone within.

Arms and legs (convincing props, even if the skin tones and blood look painted-on) fly through the air in comical curlicues, thumping against the confused and the terrified, knocking down children and drawing the attention of dogs. Teeth spatter against pavement like the spray of a wave. Knees are blown out by hammers swung with sure precision, cracking to produce guttural cries of pain and despair in all those unlucky enough to feel such sensation before death. A mummy's feet are crushed beneath the stomps of birdlike claws made of bone. Eyeballs are plucked out by skeleton-hands or speared by sharp tools wielded by the hands of the dead, the effect executed so many times that it gets better with each successive gag (you lose count). The arms are pulled off a wailing man in a *Ghostbusters* jumpsuit, trailing stringy muscle and goop.

The police are slow to react, but react they do. Drawing their pistols and raising their M4s, they spray wildly at the malignant interlopers, missing most of them, peppering the library and bystanders with deadly force, knocking down mothers and fathers and children alike, blowing holes in a portajohn and releasing its chemical toilet smell.

The Trunk or Treat is a bacchanal of chaos and murder, of horrors upon horrors indiscriminately killing everyone and everything within reach, of blood slicking along pavement and concrete, of young lives cut short or longer lives cut off, while Death itself moves through this misguided and malign community event.

While dozens have already fallen, hundreds of living bodies remain, rushing to escape the press of killers spreading throughout the crowd. But the servants of Gravedirt are ready for this. Skeletal hands (clumsy puppetry and fishing-wire movement) place barriers of dead wood, cemetery stone, graveyard rock, and sarcophagus lids along each route of egress. The earth explodes beneath the feet of the people of Canaltown, revealing more tombs, more statuary, more graves yawning open to receive the newly dead.

All avenues are cut off. There is no escape.

Save one.

Hayden spots the opening in the perimeter. Far from the center of the Trunk or Treat Carnival, he sees a narrow space between two blood-spattered armored police vehicles. He pulls Fiona forward by the hand and they duck low, knocked about by the oblivious and the terrified but remaining on their feet, because to fall would be to die, as so many small, costumed forms splattered face-first against the pavement can now attest.

They reach the vehicles—bought for cheap via a Department of Defense fire sale—and crawl between heavy, reinforced tires, pressing themselves low to avoid a rain of limbs and heads and blood as tools of agriculture are wielded in bloody harvest.

Then they scrambled beyond it all—beyond the killing, but not the screaming. They flee across the street, back across the railroad tracks, and return to the woods, hopeful that the Charred Man is not among those entities seeking their death.

Vincent Price as Charon

Along the rural outskirts of Canaltown—far from the bloody conflagration unfolding at the Trunk or Treat event—Ruthie lives alone. She almost never entertains guests, save for young Father Sutton and Deacon Brody when they make their rounds each month. But they visited just last week, and there had been no knock at the door to signal visitors, no smashing of glass or splintering of wood to announce the presence of an intruder.

She expects such chaos to occur eventually—as the television has trained her to do—and when she thinks of such things a weight rises in her chest like hands reaching up from cemetery soil to press against her heart. She often wonders if that is how death will feel, if it feels like anything.

But now there is a man sitting at her kitchen table, a man who looks very much like Vincent Price. Specifically, Vincent Price as he appeared in his role as eccentric millionaire Frederick Loren in the 1959 spookshow *House on Haunted Hill,* a film Ruthie saw at a drive-in sometime in the foggy, ill-defined decades of her receding past, and at least once on television on one of those classic movie channels around Halloween. That she remembers the name of the actor, character, and film—even the year it came out—brings a degree of pride and relief, considering the general state of her mind, of which she possesses enough faculty to recognize its slow decline.

This whole sequence looks, sounds, and feels distinct from the earlier scenes of *The Mausoleum of Gore*. The aspect ratio is bracketed by darkness above and below; the texture is more pronounced, filmed on 16mm or a reasonable facsimile; each shot is carefully composed and captured from a stationary camera position, in contrast to the run-and-gun handheld digital work of much that preceded this sequence. The actors' faces are lit with somber, warm light, their eyes glimmering with the reflection of bulbs set at multiple angles. These kitchen shots feel intimate— invasive, even— in dual medium shots and close-ups.

Like the news report, the commercials, and the journey into the arcade, this may be an add-on, an insert from a would-be cinematic Frankenstein. Is *The Mausoleum of Gore* one film, or many spliced together to form something new and vulgar? Is this formal shift part of the original scope of the project, or an unauthorized grafting-on of strange flesh?

Vincent—she is already beginning to think of him *as* Vincent Price, although that would, of course, be impossible, because that man died decades ago, lucky bastard—removes a tin of cigarettes and a set of matches from the inside breast pocket of his well-tailored black suit. Perhaps you are beginning to think of him as that famous horror film actor, too, which is a testament to the casting, the makeup, the costume work, the direction of this sequence. Or so you tell yourself. Because it could not be the *real*

Vincent Price in this bizarre, out-of-context 16mm aside in an otherwise shot-on-digital-video indie horror film you got from an acquaintance on one of the many post-Twitter social media sites that horror hounds and weird cinema freaks fled to in online diaspora.

No. Believing this to be the real, actual Vincent Price would be *fucking crazy.* And you are not fucking crazy. Ha-hah. Ha! Ah.

After placing a cigarette between his lips, Vincent strikes a match, lighting the tip and releasing a sulfuric cloud in exhale. He waves the match out and takes a few practiced, smooth pulls. Satisfied, he graces Ruthie with a smile.

"Would you join me for a smoke and a drink, my dear?" he asks, voice smooth and deep, as if he's practiced this line a hundred times before, as if you've heard him deliver it in one of his movies. "I can offer you the former, but the latter, if I may impose, would have to be provided by the host."

Ruthie nods and smiles, grateful for the opportunity to entertain. She putters over to the kitchen to search the cupboards. Darkness flees as she opens one, her face and hands probing toward the camera, finding and removing a small flask of inexpensive vodka and a green bottle of unopened Irish cream. She holds each up to her guest in the out-of-focus background, who gestures toward the cream with his cigarette, trailing smoke.

"Pour the cream over some ice in a pair of small glasses, and bring the bottle to the table. We'll have a delightful refreshment, you and I."

Ruthie closes the cabinet door and we return to darkness.

Close-up of her withered, vein-ridden hands clutching two glasses loaded with freezer-burned ice cubes, the green bottle of Irish cream tucked in the crook of her right arm. Vincent holds out a sure and steady hand to take the glasses, setting them on the table with a pleasant *clink*. Ruthie places the bottle on the table. Vincent rises and helps his host to her seat. He returns to his, canting his body in three-quarters profile, slightly reclining his great frame and lazily drawing on the cigarette. We enjoy this tableau in warm medium shot, the two sitting on either side of a pool of light that splashes against the table, bottle, and glasses, Ruthie hunched over to catch her breath, Vincent stately in his relaxed demeanor, the darkness and smoke swirling around them as void.

A swift and sure pour of the alcoholic cream splashes into each glass and the ice cubes snap in pleasant cadence. Vincent holds up his glass in toast and Ruthie raises her own to meet it. They each take a slow sip in comfortable silence. The taste on Ruthie's tongue is sweet and full, the alcohol sending a shiver of pleasure through her body. There is a flood of memories of warm summer nights, of dancing, of bodies laced with sweat, of skin and the taste of others—but they are gone swiftly, mere phantoms glanced at the end of a long, dark hallway, leaving only lingering resentment and despair like droplets of ectoplasm.

"Bill Castle was, bless his heart, always punching above his weight class," Vincent says, breaking the silence, in answer to a question unasked. He closes his eyes as he summons up his own memories, or stories about memories borrowed. "He had a great deal of talent, of course. You had to, in those days. Unlike now, when anyone can pick up a camera and call themselves a *director*. But Bill was always trying to be more than he was, to make the pictures more than they were. Not that there was anything wrong with our work together. I'm quite fond of our films, and I know that they were popular at the time and, as I'm delighted to discover, continue to be so today, among a certain subset of fans." He arrests Ruthie with a devilish grin. "Everyone likes to be scared now and again, don't they, Ruthie? If only for a moment. Oh, to be caught off guard, and then laugh, and then worry at the laugh, and to laugh at the worry."

Ruthie takes another sip. Longer, this time. *Yes, that sounds about right.*

"As an actor, I had some success and recognition, more than some, but less than I desired—or perhaps more than I deserved. Bill, he was a working man's director. I can relate to that, as I was a working actor. He was competent, on budget, on time, but he wanted more, too. Bill desired *prestige*, a Hitchcockian aura of magnificence. When he couldn't quite achieve that, he brought in the gags. Skeletons flying across the theater, buzzers under the seats, and so forth. We work with what tools we have. Perhaps in trying—and failing—to achieve true greatness, we can still achieve something memorable. Something that touches another person."

Vincent pauses to take a drag from his cigarette, then refills Ruthie's glass. He adds a splash to his own. She nods and whispers *thank you*, her words a barely audible croak.

"No, thank *you*, my dear, for the drink, for a seat to rest my bones, and for the polite company. It can be quite lonely, sometimes, you know?"

Ruthie does know.

"Being dead, I mean."

Ruthie doesn't quite know, not yet, but she has her suspicions.

"Not that I'm complaining, mind you. It's something we all must deal with, eventually, even those of wealth and privilege who have access to science and magic. Even those who have designs on escaping death's cold embrace, at great cost to themselves and others, cannot. Believe me. I have played at being those men—lingered in their minds and madness—and they never achieve what they hope to. They can only hurt others in their vain quest."

Vincent looks beyond Ruthie, focusing on something over her shoulder, on nothing at all.

"You should understand that there is a certain elemental truth in the fictions we conjure. Ripples of influence and meaning. *Occult* power. Nothing we do is in a vacuum. Nothing we think, or say, or *create* is without resonance, both outward and inward."

Ruthie shrugs. She takes another sip, feeling invigorated. How long has it been since she has had a drink with a handsome man?

"Are you enjoying our visit, Ruthie?"

She nods. Yes, she is, very much. She cannot quite follow everything Vincent is saying, but he is saying it to her, his voice is pleasant, and she is not alone. That means something.

"Do you know who I really am, Ruthie?"

Vincent Price, she says, or thinks, her words spoken in the voice of a younger woman. Her true spirit-as-self, becoming untethered, becoming aware of itself as something soon to be freed from degraded and pain-ridden flesh.

"Yes, in a manner of speaking, I am," Vincent says, smiling. "Or, rather, what he was. Those resonances summoned in his fictions. The consequences of creation, of human energy, mind and will, bouncing off the surface waters of reality, becoming something new and independent. Something *real*."

That all sounds quite interesting.

"Do you know why I'm here? Why *I* am here?"

Ruthie does not.

"You have some connection to me. To Vincent. What it is is not clear to me. I am unknowing."

I like his movies and shows. House on Haunted Hill. The Ten Commandments. Batman. *He's— you're—quite handsome, you know. And charming.*

"That is very kind, thank you. Perhaps that is reason enough. But there is a purpose to our meeting, Ruthie, beyond the pleasant social visit." Vincent leans over the table, ashing his cigarette onto a napkin. "Would you like to come with me, Ruthie? When we've finished our drinks, I mean. You see, there is something happening in town. Something *wonderful*. Something connected to the soul, or the ideas we have about souls. What is happening out there is terrifying, but it has opened up an opportunity for you. The blades of the killers and the monsters are not meant for you, as your time is nigh because of your advanced age and poor health. No goblins or demons will come creeping up to your home tonight, although others are not so lucky.

"You have a great journey ahead of you, and you do not have to take it alone. I can guide you along the path, give you encouragement. I can hold your hand, even, if that would please you. We can begin our journey into the dark at this very moment, or depart within the hour. I will leave it up to you."

One more drink, Vincent, Ruthie says, or thinks, there being no difference now. *I'm having such a lovely time visiting with you. And maybe I'll have one of your cigarettes, if you would be inclined to share?*

He smiles wide.

"I would be inclined."

He hands her the cigarette, then guides her hands up to her lips. He strikes a match and the room fills with smoke—no, *fog*, rolling in from all sides, from the dark.

"One more drink," he says, his face underlit in the encroaching darkness, pale and ghostly, soon disembodied in the deepest black, floating through the limitless beyond. "We have a little time left before the events reach their conclusion of carnage. We have a little time left before that energy is spent and we must depart..."

The Mausoleum of Gore

Back to fuzzy, handheld digital. Orange string lights and an army of jack o'lanterns reveal the forest in blazing illumination. The string lights are great strands of spider's web, crisscrossing the branches, connecting from leafless tree to leafless tree. The jack o'lanterns are legion, their eyes, noses, and mouths asymmetrical and sickly. They turn to watch Fiona and Hayden as they rush by. They turn toward the camera. To see you, and wink.

The siblings flee through intercut sequences of POV and over-the-shoulder shaky cam footage (mercifully brief) and the more artful, extreme long shot of two dark figures moving left to right through the glowing wood, rendered in paper cutout and illuminated by candlelight.

Gravedirt is too interesting a visual and movie poster draw to keep languishing off-screen for long. He pursues our leads, his heavy stone footfalls slow but sure, his scythe dripping fresh red corn syrup, his rhythmic breathing the relentless cadence of death. Whether the siblings know that the monster pursues them is irrelevant, as fear carries them (us, *you*) deeper into the uncanny.

From the malignant darkness of the forest ahead

rises a metastructure of tombs, gravestones, old wood, and ossuary-assemblage—a cancerous growth developing from shadow and branch and soil, a diagnosis-in-waiting, an eruption of foul destiny on spoiled flesh that heralds the end, the end of all things, because when a person dies, the whole world dies with them, and many people and many worlds have died and will die and are dying, even right now, even you and yours. Even you and yours.

These disparate elements form and reform, their elemental properties rearranging from dead bones, soil, fallen branches, and leaves into planks of black wood, slathered in cheap paint and crookedly assembled. A facade of a house, shimmering and glowing blackly under a harvest moon, built from the very miasma of *Halloween* and *haunted house* and *forbidden space* as drawn from the minds of Hayden and Fiona, drawn from mine, drawn from yours. String lights blink to life, popping up like pustules. Greens, purples, oranges, and blacklights.

Fiona recognizes this place first—rather, she recognizes this as a *type* of place and, in sensing its nature, knows that they must enter. The only way out of horror is through, after all.

Spookhouse. That is the word for it. A childish name, dredging up memories of Dr. Vampire's House of Horrors, a rickety, ancient attraction that lingered at the edge of the county fairgrounds in the old days, when she was growing up, five, six years ago. Ancient history. Back when rubber masks and the static-ridden squealing of goblins and the cackling of witches from hidden speakers could frighten and thrill. Back when the horrors of the real world merely lingered at the periphery, like moving shadows cast by figures unseen. Older now, wiser, she is beginning to understand that the real horrors are not mummies and vampires in spooky, isolated haunted houses. The really scary things are part of the fabric of life. They come to you.

Above the sagging roof of the porch overhang is a great, wide sign of crooked wood. The paint that announces the name of the attraction is bright orange and red, highlighted with splattered colors that glow in the blacklight:

THE MAUSOLEUM OF GORE

Fiona takes the first step forward.

Her brother starts to speak up, but the words die in his throat. He understands as she does. Because to resist—to deny death as the final spookhouse ride that we must all take—leads to madness, to true and terrible sin.

Why horror?

Because nothing else will suffice.

Wooden doors bang open. A rattling cart rolls out on metal tracks, slamming to a halt in the dead center of the porch. Overhead lights, blood red, flicker on with a caustic buzz. The high-backed cart is hand painted with big-eyed bats and wispy white ghosts shaped by the strokes of a cheap, wide paintbrush. There's room enough for two.

Fiona lifts the metal safety bar and gets into the cart. She shuffles to the far side. Hayden hangs back.

"Come on," Fiona says. A scream, echoing to them from deep in the woods, encourages him, too.

Death bears down, regardless of the choices we make. We may as well enjoy the ride.

Hayden makes his choice, then, or the illusion of one. He steps into the cart. He searches for a seat belt or restraint and, finding none, allows a bark of a laugh at such an absurdity. After a moment of quiet, another scream sounds throughout the forest. Closer. Perhaps others escaped the carnage of the parking lot killing field, too, if only for a time.

"Why isn't it moving?" Fiona asks.

Hayden's fumbling hands find a boxy, metal protrusion fastened to the cart's front panel. A light above them hisses to life, spraying a yellowed cone of illumination upon the device in revelation: a pair of speakers and a tape deck. Thick, teeth-like buttons sit along its surface. Hayden presses one and the tape door pops open, trailing cobweb strands of saliva and coughing up a plume of corpse-dust.

Fiona produces the cassette tape gifted by the card reader. *Spooky Sounds from a Haunted House* fits inside. She presses the door closed. One of the buttons on top is marked with a fingerprint in blood, long since dried. It clicks down with the snap of a rotten tooth.

The speakers crackle and spark. The cart lurches forward, metal wheels on metal rails squealing. The cassette player produces a low, thrumming, semi-musical track. Chains jingle in the soft breeze of a forgotten, subterranean tunnel. The dead moan in anguish, vaguely syllabic half-words stretching across the aural space. A pipe organ produces sonorous notes, low and spooky: the forgotten, heat-damaged soundtrack to a lost Gothic horror film.

As the cart slams through the swinging entrance doors of the Mausoleum of Gore—hand-painted, bloodshot eyes irradiating green waves of menace—a voice moans, as if disturbed from a fitful dream.

"We are...we are so glad you can join us for this journey tonight," the voice says, masculine and sonorous. Vincent, perhaps, returning for one last performance this evening. Pages rustle and ice clinks against the limits of a glass. The cart rolls through a dark tunnel illuminated by blacklight and spattered by reflective paint, evoking crime-scene spoor. "Welcome to the Mausoleum of Gore. A haunted house of ill repute, a blasted mansion of deviltry and madness, a home to wonder and horror in equal measure."

Ghostly figures in covered sheets move back and forth across the track ahead. Fiona and Hayden grip the metal handlebars.

"We hope you enjoy the ride. It may be your last. Muah, ha, ha, haaaaaaah—" The laughter stretches out into reverberating distortion, subsumed by the thrumming of a low-tempo synthesizer score. Off-brand Goblin by way of a church organ player on acid.

As the cart rattles closer to the ghosts passing through slats of blue light ahead, the sheet-covered spirits move in rhythm with the music bleeding through the speakers. Hayden and Fiona brace for a jump scare—for actors or animatronics in white sheets to leap forward, arms outstretched. Recesses hold the ghosts in shadow—figures inverted, standing (floating?) on the ceiling, some trick of mirror and light, maybe.

"No tricks here," the voice on the tape says. "Just treats. Nocturnal delights. The wonders of the world of the dead."

Fiona lets out a shriek. A hand—no arm, no actor, just a *hand*—wrapped in gauze and alive with blue light, releases itself from her shoulder, then raises up in a friendly wave as the cart rattles onward.

"They—they shouldn't touch us," Hayden says, as if that means anything.

"It was cold," Fiona says rubbing at her shoulder. White-sheet ghosts materialize next to the floating hand, waving goodbye to the living on their journey. As the cart rolls on they fade away, becoming vapor, devoured by the dark.

The cart passes through a set of doors with brown wooden slats and sparkling glass handles. They roll into a cramped living room with walls of velvet red. A rectangular dining table and hand-carved wooden chairs hang from the ceiling. Skeleton props remain seated, motors whirring to move arm bones and clack jaws, giving the impression of undeath. The cart passes beneath. Pots of stinking liquid are smoking and boiling overhead. Mounds of spaghetti noodles vibrate and squirm. Silverware rattles, held aloft by anti-gravitational forces. The riders' hair rises, and they must grip the metal bar to keep from floating out of the cart completely.

"Pass the eyeballs," the voice on the tape says, the music adopting a whimsical, low tone. Right on cue, a skeleton pivots to pass a bowl of glistening, gelatinous eyes freshly plucked from screaming faces, directly overhead. One breaks free from the cluster to fall and spatter against the side of the cart before rolling off to the track below, leaving a trail of clear slime.

The lights go out and the world is dark.

Wood on wood, sliding and striking. The clattering of wheels against the track. The hum of unseen machinery, remaking the world anew.

Television sets alight in the near distance. A blast of cold air. The drumming of static through the speakers. The screens are stacked in three columns, bulbous and asymmetrical. The static gives way to black and white footage, crosshairs at the center of the screen, alphanumeric codes shifting at the edges. Those crosshairs descend and center on illuminated silhouettes of people gathered together. A spray of vibrant light from behind the camera, and the people collapse or disintegrate. A car explodes. The wall of a building collapses. Some of the screens shift to cell phone footage of wailing women in long, dark clothing and facial coverings, hands likewise covered not in fabric but in blood. Men rush through a crowded street, carrying a body between them— another man who can't be more than twenty years old—covered in blood. Limp forms of children, eyes open, pressed to the chests of their wailing fathers. Other children and teenagers standing still, spattered with white dust and blood, eyes wide, faces bloodied, lives crushed, the future a dead horizon.

A production line of a US aerospace contractor factory, perhaps like the one just down the highway from Canaltown, New York, where technicians in white lab cloaks hover over material components, conducting inspections and ensuring everything proceeds as planned. Carnage on export, directed by men and women in nice suits in flat, soulless boardrooms. Close-ups of vegan and gluten-free options provided as part of the catering package for expensive team-building exercises. Free-trade coffee, two types of cream, including nondairy option. A pile of plastic and foam in the garbage to be collected by the underpaid facilities staff and ultimately dumped in the ocean. PowerPoint slides cycling through the banalities of empire: profit reports, ominous warnings of wage increases, updates on donations to major public research universities to sponsor ethics courses.

The television screens fill with fake blood, because the designer of this particular gag isn't interested in subtlety. The screens spark and gurgle, overflowing with Technicolor orange-red liquid. A girl's voice calls out alphanumeric strings in cadence, the soft jingle of an ice cream truck underpinning her half-words, soon replaced by the drone of a church organ score to a Spanish-produced horror film from the 1970s.

The track curves away and toward another set of swinging doors. A blood-spattered message, riddled with paint that catches the blacklight, glows in the speech bubble of a malignant, ghostly figure with a bag over its head:

THE WHOLE WORLD IS A CRYPT OF BLOOD

An American flag drops from the ceiling in proper jump-scare, hanging just above the cart. The tape plays a tinny rendition of "Taps." A spotlight illuminates Old Glory, revealing its red stripes to be fresh blood, spilling down across the crossbars of white, dripping down upon the riders' heads as they pass beneath in blasphemous baptism. On the other side, the ghost's message has inexplicably changed:

MAMMON IS A GENEROUS GOD
BLESSINGS BOUGHT WITH MASS MURDER

The cart slams into the door, kicking up specks of fresh paint (BLOOD) and pressing further into darkness.

One Good Scare

There is more. Rooms upon rooms of animatronic and costumed horrors; snippets of familiar horror film soundtracks played at odd intervals and tempos; long stretches of dark, empty tunnels when the voice on the tape murmurs inaudibly, cries, or simply begs for its life.

A ghost-faced killer from a long-running movie franchise wields a chainsaw and revs it over Fiona's head. A wall of sharp, protruding bones like the open jaws of a giant, predatory animal threatens to slam down onto their shaky cart. A chamber bathed in blue light is home to a massive, tubular creature, shifting and gurgling, its distended bulk threatening to spill into the corridor and crush them. A slaughterhouse is replete with hanging carcasses dripping with blood, their malformed shapes not recognizably animal. A hollow void yawns open for them on all sides, the air icy and cutting, with only the rickety track remaining solid. A pumpkin-headed humanoid with roots and stems twisted into limbs wields an axe and dismembers dead-eyed victim-mannequins in gleeful geysers of blood. In a hall of mirrors, each new reflection offers a glimpse of a different set of traumas, injuries, or disease ravaging their frail and wasted bodies in hologram.

The cart pushes through a set of doors into a great open space, a room unlike the others. The air is cool, and the walls pull back to reveal a vast stretch of forest. Pine trees stretch high to the elevated ceiling. Painted stars glimmer between dancing boughs. Pools of darkness and purposefully aimed cones of light guide the eye to a footpath that leads away from the uneven track.

"This is the end of the line, end of the track, end of the spookshow," Vincent's voice warbles. "That thing is in pursuit, and will soon reach you. You haven't much time. If you want to see, you will have to walk. Or you can wait. Wait for death to take you. It's all the same, to us…"

The tape ends, the device clicking to a halt. Brimstone puffs out of the speakers.

The cart rattles forward another few feet, then comes to a squealing halt at the edge of the trail into the faux forest.

Hayden steps out first. The ground is moist and giving under his feet, like real earth and forest grass. The air smells of mud and pine. Fiona pulls herself out of the cart, just before it rolls forward again, disappearing around a bend of grey rocks and a tangle of downed trees whose roots writhe in the air.

Fog creeps up against the path, glowing soft and viridian—disquieting and inviting in equal measure. They walk for some time, listening for the clamber and crunch of machinery but hearing only the wind and the rustle of branches shedding their remaining leaves. This place feels wild and open, and the trees, dirt, grass, and rocks all look real—or, in the soft glow of the creeping fog holding close to the ground, *more real than real.*

They follow the trail, at the mercy of its design. Soon a structure reveals itself in orange ridges and columns of vine. A massive, bulbous jack o'lantern looms at the end of the path, the size of a witch's hut. Its eyes and nasal cavity are clumsy triangles, carved by an unpracticed but enthusiastic hand. The path leads directly to its great, open mouth, where its flat rectangle teeth part to allow them entrance. Candlelight glows in pleasant waves of amber. Inside, the chamber is warmed by a multitude of white candles, all burning low and soft, set on silver plates and hand-carved wooden stands, or within bronze lanterns with flat glass windows. Two chairs wait at the center of the space, set before a stone altar over which a cloaked skeleton lies slumped.

The chairs slide back and, well beyond any sense of self-preservation or question, Hayden and Fiona take their seats in a disquieting echo of their visit to the Tarot card reader. In fact, the skeleton wears a robe quite like hers, but hole-ridden and dirt-encrusted. The gold inlay is faded and frayed.

There's no running. There never is. The fortune teller. The Charred Man. Vincent Price. Many voices as one, modulated and mixed together for unnerving effect.

Make an offering. Something for the ghosts and goblins.

Fiona reaches a shaking hand into her bag, her eyes on the skeleton, expecting it to move, to reach out and grab her. She retrieves a handful of small chocolate bars and sets them in the center of the table, sure that the skeleton's death grip will seize her by the wrist.

And for you. Something for yourselves.

She hands her brother a bite-sized piece and keeps one for herself. She tears off the wrapper, her eyes never leaving the still, deathly form slumped before her.

Always check your candy, the voice(s) say. *Your people created fear of a holiday meant to acknowledge fear. Isn't that something? How deep does the death-drive in your culture go, that it cannot engage in a ritualized process meant to alleviate fear about the inevitable without creating additional neuroses? That you would rather suffer in sublimated terror, rather than laugh, and eat, and drink, and be merry? You could frolic in brine, goblins be thine, for one night a year, no consequences, no questions asked. But no. No, parents must gift terrors to their children. Because the world you have built for yourselves is a gaping wound, bleeding out. A nation of fear, whose violence is projected outward and inward in ever-increasing waves. How long until it all comes crashing down?*

A finger on the skeleton's hand wiggles. Or Fiona imagines it does.

She looks down at the chocolate she holds between her fingers. She doesn't like this kind so much—all that cheap caramel sticks to her teeth—but candy is candy, and she can sense her opportunity to trick-or-treat slipping further away every year. Already, many of her classmates and friends loudly declare that they are too old, too *mature* to go trick-or-treating. Others still go, sure, but they eschew costumes for hoodies and sweatpants. How long until she joins either group, resisting the spirit by participating in half-measure, or turning from the dark path of pilgrimage completely?

No razor blades. No nails. No tacks. No broken glass. No hypodermic needles. It's just a piece of cheap chocolate, like any other.

Well. We stand on tradition here, and tradition that has become.

Fiona and Hayden take the first tentative bites of their candy. They are both caught off guard by the taste. Their reactions are captured in murky close-up, eyes wide, white light trained on them from below for spooky emphasis. The candy is fresher, sweeter. It tastes the way it used to taste, back when they were younger, when their senses were sharper and caramel and chocolate could trigger an innocent ecstasy. Those pure sensations and experiences have all but washed away down a river of time, chased off before the oncoming march of adulthood, of disappointment, of losses to come.

I was wondering when you would show up.

A head, trailing its spinal cord, rolls into the tent. NINA VAN HORN, VILLAGE COUNCIL, in bloody close-up. Face smeared in grey makeup, red paint-as-blood smeared along the flaps of her neck flesh.

"I'm not really dead," she croaks, watery blood gushing over her teeth. "This is all some sort of sick gag." She struggles to wink, the muscles in her face already seizing up. "Uh-oh! Here comes trouble." She rolls back out of the pumpkin hollow in reversed shot.

Forest exterior: Gravedirt stomping through the darkness, the fog parting for him. Stone, soil, and tufts of grass piled into human form, the ghoulish golem halting between the candlelight that spills from the great jack o'lantern and the synthetic darkness of the forest.

Play Halloween games, win Halloween prizes.

The robed skeleton at the table shuffles a deck of cards. Another Tarot deck. The backs of the cards are adorned with the iconography of Halloween: black cats and witches, children in handmade ghost and goblin costumes, fields of corn at sunset, neon-green vampire fangs, a television screen showing *Night of the Living Dead*, plastic skeletons waving from leaf-strewn front lawns. Halloween is yours, too. What else is on the cards? What does it all mean to *you*, specifically? You see that, too. The good and the bad. The comforting and the terrifying, holiday memories past and yet to come.

One more reading. One card for each of you.

Overhead close-up of the table, two cards facedown. Interference rumbles across the screen, revealing the ghost of footage taped over and replaced. There are glimpses of a stage, of coffin props, of rubber bats. Of fire. There is a shot of a dark figure that looms in the near distance, planks of alien light silhouetting it. Its head raises to reveal curled horns. It wields a mass of wet metal, a blood-spattered chainsaw in outline. Errant stretches of Halloween decoration B-roll; costumed customers in line for a nightmare hayride; cheap-looking ghouls breaking into a barricaded manor in some Euroschlock zombie movie.

Gravedirt waits, stone and soil heaving with false breath in the dark.

Reveal your fate.

Hayden reaches forward and turns over the card on the left.

A skull, with black hood drawn up, framed by the blade of a scythe that hangs above.

Death. And you, child.

Fiona reaches a quivering hand up to the card. The sound of skin on paper, the rustling of a specter outside your bedroom door.

Twin grim reapers revealed, smiling flatly from the table.

Death for you as well.

Fiona reaches over her chair to grab her brother in a desperate embrace. He allows himself to return the hug. She presses her face into his shoulder.

Laughter. The skeleton's voice warping and crackling with static, as if played from the Halloween tape. It fixes them in place with empty eye sockets fluttering with spectral green light. A spectral underpinning of somber organ horror movie music rises. Toccata and Fugue in D Minor.

This is the way of all flesh. Your essential mind— your spirit, the true essence of yourself beyond the limits of flesh and sinly nature—are bound for a country yet unknown. Wide and endless. And wonderful.

"But how do we know that?" Hayden says, aware that Gravedirt has taken another step closer to the jack o'lantern. Closer to them. There's a *shing* sound effect and an intercut flash of metal as its blood-dripping scythe is brought to bear for the camera's benefit.

Hayden grips Fiona all the tighter.

"We can't know that. No matter what you say."

"We don't even know what you *are*," Fiona says, finding anger in her fear and latching onto it.

That's all part of the fun, isn't it? The not-knowing. The fear. It's Halloween, children. Everyone is entitled to one good scare. Let the promise of death, and the uncertainty of what lies beyond, be mine, for you. My scare. My gift.

The bulky killer of stone and dirt steps forward. They lower their malformed head beneath the teeth of the great jack o'lantern to enter. Fiona presses into Hayden's side, and he allows a single tear for them both.

As Gravedirt passes over the threshold, chunks of stone roll off their body to land against the moist flesh of the floor. Headstone fragments shatter and collapse. Dirt pours out of cracks in the stone and from tufts of dead grass. Their scythe, held aloft for the killing blow just moments prior, tumbles forward to embed itself point-first into the surface of the table. Its strong wooden handle is suspended in the air, just above Hayden and Fiona.

The skeleton opens its jaw as if to laugh. But it falls away, tumbling harmlessly onto the table, landing atop the Death cards. A low moan, tinged with electronic wash, flutters up to the top of the jack o'lantern, and is gone.

The skeleton slumps forward, striking the frontispiece of its skull against the curve of the scythe blade and cracking open. Dust pours out of its ruined robe, now fraying. The smell of vegetation—a cornfield left unharvested in November—overpowers the air.

Gravedirt tries to step forward, but with each passing moment, more of their stone, dirt, branch, vine, and statuary loses coherency. They are becoming as sand, disintegrating like a vampire in the sunlight.

The candles blow out, one by one.

The jack o'lantern withers and sags. Fiona holds tight to her bag of candy and, for a reason she does not fully understand, grabs the two Death cards, too, careful not to touch the blood-drenched scythe. She slips the cards into her bag. She and her brother step over the still-crumbling remains of Gravedirt and leave the rotting jack o'lantern before its mouth falls closed.

Graves explode up and out of the forest floor—not some special effect operated by hydraulics, but coming up through the spookhouse's underlying structure, breaking through the artifice of wood and black paint, disrupting the natural and the synthetic alike. Falsehood and construct, truth and nature, collapsing and rotting away. The stars above glitter and glow orange, then blink out. Trees shake and lift their roots from false earth, then leverage their trunks like battering rams to smash against hidden walls and painted hills and false stretches of forest. Real trees stand in orange moonlight, visible through the wounds battered in the spookhouse walls which moan and collapse.

The cart tracks disappear under quicksand. The walls and chambers and horrors of The Mausoleum of

Gore are subsumed by the true forest and the true night, pulled down into the earth like a million generations of people and proto-people before and to come. The stage shall be swept clean and reset. There is another performance scheduled soon, and another after that, and both the living and the dead shall have their parts to play, as they always do, as you always have and always will, until the very end, which is no end at all but merely intermission.

The forest night and its stars are revealed through the great tearing and ripping apart of the false firmament. Those stars are real, or as real as they need be for this part of the movie. Buzzing and ominous.

As the last stretches of wall and falsehood of the mausoleum rot and collapse away, the distant lights of Canaltown act as guiding stars. Fiona's bag of candy offers a pleasant susurrus of plastic and candy wrappers.

They reach the edge of the forest. Across the road is the municipal parking lot and the remnants of the carnage of the Trunk or Treat Carnival. Bodies are strewn among hundreds of jack o'lanterns, faces carved into monsters real and imaginary.

Death is a jealous god, and will not suffer being forgotten. Even if the spirit endures, the flesh fails. And that is good, because that is its purpose, and what lies beyond...

One voice as many, speaking through the dim crackle of a haunted house soundtrack tape, speaking at the edge of the wind, along the rustling of swirling leaves, through the laughter of children trick-or-treating.

Soon will return cold, sweet autumn air. Soon will return early sunsets and the howl of coyotes, the hooting of owls, and black cats chasing impossible shadows. Soon will death return, restored to its proper place of honor, of warning, of holy and natural purpose.

The massacred dead arise.

The voice deepens, becoming richer, louder, clearer, spoken from the darkness just over your shoulder:

Thank you for watching The Mausoleum of Gore: A Halloween TV Special. *Be sure to tell others of what you have seen. Be sure to remember the good and proper lessons in moral hygiene and spiritual reverence imparted by these images of societal decay and meaningless violence. Recall in earnest the soft caress of autumn air and the taste of rich candy and the warm, inner glow you experience when watching a creaky horror picture on a quiet, grey October weekend afternoon. Worry not that this film (BOOK) might not be found in your possession when you summon the courage to share it with another, for it appears only to those whom it has chosen, and only when the time is right. You will know. You will know. And so will they.*

Your time has been right, but now, your time is at an end. All times, all lives. End.

A Note from the Filmmakers

A flash of static. Searing blue light gives way to a soft, comforting shade as your eyes adjust. Fuzzy text in a flat, white typeface against the blue background scrolls up your computer screen:

THIS HORROR PICTURE'S CAST AND CREW WISH TO THANK:

- The victims and perpetrators of generational trauma in and around Canaltown, New York

- The SUNY Canaltown English and Cinema Department—especially the student worker who let us sign the camera equipment out over the weekends and didn't charge us extra!!

- Christopher Leaf and Peter Cushman (weed joke)

- Mary and Madeleine Collinson (😍 😍)

- Barbara Steele-our-Hearts (😍 😍 😍)

- The **CHARRED MAN** for divine revelations shared over rolling clouds of The King in Yellow smoke

☻ All ufological and associated goblin phenomena that occurred the summer of 2022 in Ellicottville, New York (IT IS REAL BUT THE GOVERNMENT "DISCLOSURE" IS FAKE)

☻ The restless spirits of Dan O'Bannon and Jean Rollin for their sound advice and ominous warnings From Beyond

☻ The Auteur, producers, cast, and crew (and resonating black-pyramidal structures) from *The Secret Goatman Spookshow* who generously contributed their time, expertise, and psychic energies to this production, and for introducing us to the "Cinema Goblin" school of filmmaking

☻ Malthus International Arts & Sciences Philanthropic Trust for the noncompetitive and unsolicited creatives grant (we bought a TON of weed and beer with the money)

☻ AND VIEWERS LIKE YOU!!!!

HAPPY HALLOWEEN

Black.

Hold on black.

Hold for a long time.

Hold until you're *just* about to stop playback, to "x" out of the video player program and find something else to do with the rapidly dwindling time you have left before the grave.

Black finally gives way to the top ridges of a pumpkin, softly illuminated by flickering candlelight. A carved eye—a crooked, downward-sloping triangle—is just barely visible in the lower righthand corner of the screen. A dull, green glow flickers within, sputtering on the edge of death and darkness. Shimmering, fading, and indistinct, the jack o'lantern reemerges from shadow and fog as a skull, now center frame, jaw open and eye sockets alight with nauseating green fire.

Stock horror typeface, bloody and red, stroke lines of neon green light spilling into our world, pulses across the screen as we dolly in to the skull:

THE TRILOGY OF FOUND-FOOTAGE METAHORROR CONCLUDES IN

THE OSSUARY OF DOOM
A HALLOWEEN TV SPECIAL

About the Contributors

Jonathan Raab is the author of *Project Vampire Killer*, *The Haunting of Camp Winter Falcon*, *The Crypt of Blood: A Halloween TV Special*, and more. He is the designer of the *Vampyrvania* tabletop roleplaying game and edited the anthologies *Euroschlock Nightmares*, *Behold the Undead of Dracula*, and *Terror in 16-Bits*. His short fiction has appeared in numerous magazines and anthologies, including *The Best Horror of the Year*, Volume Fourteen. He lives in Gothic upstate New York with his wife and son.

Artist/musician **Mat Fitzsimmons** has contributed graphics to the underground (music posters; surf, skate, snowboard art; punk 'zines; independent books) for over 25 years, along with fronting the savage rock juggernaut, Herbert/Automatic Animal (1993-2018). A life-long resident, Fitz lives in Santa Cruz, CA with wife Brandi & giant cat Chloe, where he draws inspiration from the shadows of the mountains to the depths of the sea.
Contact: feralteethpress@gmail.com.

Trevor Henderson is a writer, illustrator, and creature concept artist. His love of monsters, cryptids, ghosts, and other malevolent entities is enduring and vast. He recently wrote and illustrated a scary chapter book for middle-grade readers called *Scarewaves*, and he was the sole creature concept artist for the horror film *Tarot*. When he is not drawing or writing horrible things, he is probably watching an old Italian horror film or playing with his cat named Boo. He lives in Toronto with his partner, Jenn.

Steve Grinstead walked away from a perfectly respectable career as managing editor for History Colorado, but he still spends his time editing books, magazine features, and exhibitions. Recent titles he has edited include *Super Indian: Fritz Scholder 1967–1980* and Jonathan Raab's previous novel, *Project Vampire Killer*. He is the coauthor of *Walking Into Colorado's Past: 50 Front Range History Hikes*, winner of the Colorado Book Award for Nonfiction. He lives in Denver and Salida with his wife, Leigh.